Colm & the
Lazarus
Key

Kieran Mark Crowley

Colm & the Lazarus Key

MERCIER PRESS
Irish Publisher – Irish Story

MERCIER PRESS

Cork

www.mercierpress.ie

Trade enquiries to CMD,
55a Spruce Avenue, Stillorgan Industrial Park,
Blackrock, County Dublin

© Kieran Mark Crowley, 2009

ISBN: 978 1 85635 646 6

10 9 8 7 6 5 4 3 2 1

A CIP record for this title is available from the British Library

This book is sold subject to the condition that it shall not, by way of trade or otherwise, be lent, resold, hired out or otherwise circulated without the publisher's prior consent in any form of binding or cover other than that in which it is published and without a similar condition including this condition being imposed on the subsequent purchaser.

No part of this publication may be reproduced or transmitted in any form or by any means, electronic or mechanical, including photocopying, recording or any information or retrieval system, without the prior permission of the publisher in writing.

All characters, locations and events in this book are entirely fictional. Any resemblance to any person, living or dead, which may occur inadvertently is completely unintentional.

Printed and bound in the EU.

Mercier Press receives
financial assistance from
the Arts Council/An
Chomhairle Ealaíon

For Jessica

The world's greatest niece.

and for Dee

Thanks for all your love and support, for reading
the chapters late into the night, and for the seven
hundred and twenty-one times you said, 'go to your
desk and get writing'. You were right – it wasn't
nagging, it was encouragement.

Special thanks to Mam, D.J., Deirdre and Fiona.

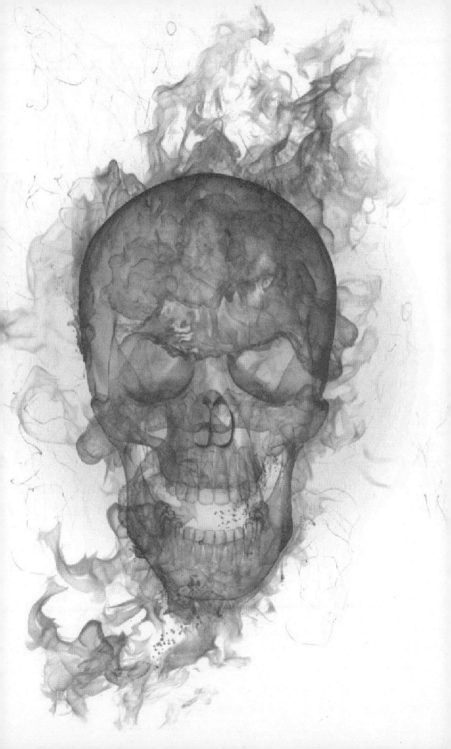

One

The little red car rattled around the bend at forty-three kilometres per hour. Colm, who was squashed into the back seat alongside The Brute, made a quick calculation. At this speed they'd reach his aunt's house in two hours and seventeen minutes. In less than two and a half hours The Brute would be out of his life forever.

The Brute was Michael James McGrath, Colm's first cousin, Aunt Deirdre's little boy, as Colm's mother called him. Little wasn't exactly the right word to describe him. Ants were little. Bonsai trees were little. Chihuahuas were little. Michael was big. No, not big, huge. He was three years older than Colm, over a foot taller and two stone heavier. Colm wouldn't have minded if it was two stone of fat. Fat he could deal with; he wasn't exactly slim himself. But The Brute was pure muscle.

None of that mattered now. The longest fortnight of his short life was almost over. It had been exactly fourteen days since The Brute had arrived at Colm's home, a sneer on his lips and a battered sports bag slung over his shoulder. Aunt Deirdre and her second husband, Bald Seanie, were in Lanzarote for their honeymoon and Michael had been dumped on Colm's family. To make matters worse, because the house was so small he had to sleep in Colm's room. He had even been given Colm's bed – 'he is a guest, after all' – while Colm had the choice of a sleeping bag on the floor or the couch that stank of his father's socks.

Reasons why Colm disliked The Brute:

1. When he slept he either snored or let go of some immense rippers; on the bad nights he did both at the same time. As his mother said, 'He's fond of bum belches.' She thought that giving it a polite name made it easier to put up with, but she didn't have to live with the smell.

2. Every single morning he punched Colm on his left shoulder. This was his 'daily dig'. He wasn't happy until huge purple and yellow bruises had formed on Colm's shoulder like a badly drawn tattoo.

3. When he first saw Colm's large collection of books he looked confused and asked: 'Why do you have

so many books? Is your television broken?' Then he
called him a girl and gave him his very first 'daily dig'.

4. When he wasn't punching or snoring or ripping, he
    picked his nose and either ate what he excavated or
    flicked it at Colm's head.

5. During the week, he had come up with a lot of
    nicknames for Colm. Random sample of nicknames:
    Pygmy (partly true; Colm was small for his age);
    Weasel Features (just plain mean); Rancid Reject
    (made no sense).

He also boasted. About the number of goals he scored every
time he played a hurling match. About the number of fights
he won in school until he had to stop fighting because he
was going to be thrown out. And about girls. Mostly, he
boasted about girls.

The Brute: Number of Girlfriends – 32; Number of Kisses
– 39

Colm: Number of Girlfriends – 0; Number of Kisses
– ½

After the first night, when his mother asked him how they
were getting on, Colm told her that they didn't have much
in common. She said that he'd have to try harder. Maybe
she's right, he'd thought. They had to have something that
connected them other than blood.

They didn't.

The car turned onto the main road. The speedometer showed they were now travelling at sixty-one kilometres per hour. This was quite fast for Colm's father. He didn't like driving and avoided sitting behind the steering wheel whenever he could. He always cycled to work, jeans' legs tucked into his socks and, much to his wife's horror, his shirt tucked into his underpants.

'Keeps out the cold,' he'd say, by way of explanation.

But since Michael lived in a small village on the coast that wasn't served by either rail or bus, he had no choice other than to drive.

Usually journeys with his parents were quiet and peaceful. Colm would sit in the back of the car reading a book, while his mam asked his dad questions from a quiz book. His dad almost always got all the answers right. They'd had a quiz earlier, but had given up when The Brute kept distracting them.

Question: What type of acid is the main acid in your stomach?

Dad: Hydrochloric Acid.

The Brute: Aunt Acid.

Question: Which is the largest of the apes?

Dad: Silverback Gorilla.

The Brute: King Kong.

After that the journey had taken place mainly in silence.

Colm's father took a deep breath and gripped the steering wheel tightly, his knuckles turning white, as he prepared to overtake a tractor. It was only when they were safely past that he breathed out again.

'You were just like James Bond there, Uncle Joe,' said Michael.

Oh yeah, The Brute was also sarcastic. Colm didn't mind that too much – sarcasm was better than a dig in the arm any day – but his parents hated it. They'd bitten their tongues a lot over the course of the first week as they knew it couldn't have been easy for Michael to spend some of his holidays with a family he barely knew, but they could only be polite for so long, especially his father. He'd made a promise to his wife not to say anything nasty to Michael, so whenever he got annoyed with his nephew he just left the room until he'd cooled down. He couldn't do that now. He was trapped.

The bald patch on the back of his father's head turned red, a sure sign that his temper was rising, but before he could say anything, his mobile phone jerked into life with its chirpy U2 ring tone. Colm hated that ring tone. He had been with his father in the car park in Dunnes once when the mobile rang, just as two of the lads from his class sloped past. Dads weren't meant to have musical ring tones. They were meant to have the boring ring-ring or the default

Nokia setting. It was an unwritten law. And when Paddy and Iano heard the phone's pitiful tune and spotted Colm, it was instant public embarrassment followed by days of slagging in school about his pathetic old man. Just what he needed. He'd tried to explain to his dad that he shouldn't have such a ring tone at his age, but his dad wasn't having any of it. When it came to anything to do with U2, there was no talking to him. He'd been a few years behind Bono in school and regarded him as a personal friend even though they'd never even spoken.

'U2 is the best band in the world and if your friends can't see that then they're fools,' was his final word on the matter.

Luckily, his classmates tired of slagging him soon enough and found someone else to tear into, but Colm still prayed that none of them would ever see his dad cycling his old racer to work. They'd never let up if they copped on to that one.

'Answer the phone, Mary,' his father said through gritted teeth.

Colm's mother pressed the answer button.

'Hello. Oh, Deirdre, how are you? We're just on the way to ...'

Her tone swiftly changed from cheery to frosty. She wasn't happy.

'No, of course not. That's no problem at all. Do you want to speak to Michael? OK. See you then.'

She ended the call and turned to Michael with a smile that didn't reach her eyes.

'That was your mother.'

'Yeah,' said The Brute, acting cool.

She hadn't phoned her son directly because he'd flung his mobile against the bedroom wall when he was angry and it hadn't worked since. Mobiles usually didn't when they were smashed into fifteen different pieces.

'They missed their flight, but they'll be able to get one in the morning.'

'Oh.'

Colm wasn't certain, but he thought he saw The Brute's lower lip quiver. Was it possible that this creature had emotions hidden behind that blank face of his? Did he actually miss his mother? For the briefest of moments he almost felt sorry for him. He offered up what he thought was a sympathetic smile. His cousin looked at him and said, 'What are you laughing at, you fat-headed clown?'

Sympathy over. Twenty-four more hours with The Brute. Fantastic.

•◆•

Twenty minutes later they were eating greasy burgers in silence, as the traffic roared past the roadside café. Empty plastic chairs shook whenever a lorry trundled by, which was about once every thirty seconds.

'What are we going to do, Dad?'

'We'll just have to go back home, I suppose,' Colm's father said, as he picked at the piece of onion that was stuck in his back teeth.

His mother snorted. It was a sound she rarely made, but one which Colm and his father never liked to hear. It meant that she was cross. They silently chewed on their burgers. Both of them hoped that by ignoring her, she might forget what had annoyed her. It was a trick they often used. As usual, it failed.

'Back home?' she said in a voice so icy you could have used it to chill a warm glass of Coke.

Colm's father paused before he spoke, choosing every word carefully.

'What else can we do? Sure, Michael's parents ...'

'Seanie's not my dad,' The Brute interrupted, through a mouthful of curly fries.

'Michael's mam and his stepfather won't be home for at least a day. We don't have a key to their place, so we can't stay there. We might as well go home.'

'I could break in,' said The Brute. 'You could leave me there. I'd be fine on my own.'

'That's an option,' Colm's father said.

'No, it's not,' said his mother. 'The boy is far too young to stay by himself.'

'I don't mind,' The Brute said.

'You're not staying on your own,' she replied in a voice that meant the argument was over.

'What are we going to do then?' Colm's father asked.

'We could stay in a hotel. Make a weekend of it. Have a bit of an adventure.'

'No way,' he said. He hated sleeping in any bed other than his own.

His wife gave him a dirty look. When it came to dirty looks she was up there with the best of them.

'I said no and I mean no,' he said, although his voice was a little shaky. 'We're not going to a hotel and that's my last word on the matter. I'm putting my foot down.'

His foot remained down for fourteen minutes before he gave in and they began to look for a hotel. Colm's mother didn't like the first one they found. She said it was soulless. Colm wasn't sure what she meant, but it was big and unwelcoming and he didn't like the look of it either. The second hotel was rejected due to the litter that swirled around the car park.

'If it's filthy on the outside, you can imagine what it's like on the inside,' his mother had said.

The third hotel was just right. The driveway was long

and winding, and the gravel crunched beneath the car tyres. It was bordered by large, neatly trimmed hedges sprinkled with September lily.

'This is more like it,' she said.

The driveway opened out into a large courtyard and they got their first look at the Red House Hotel (although it was really more of a large country house than a hotel). It was three storeys high with old-fashioned windows that had been installed long before double-glazing had been invented. Ivy crept along the stone walls.

'Looks a bit posh,' said Colm's father. When he said posh, he meant that he was worried it would cost a lot of money to stay there.

'It's not open,' The Brute said, but nobody paid any attention.

'There's a sign on the door.'

'Colm, get out and have a look, like a good man. See what it says.'

Colm got out of the car. He smelled pine in the air. Must be coming from the forest, he thought. The courtyard was surrounded by trees that were at least a hundred years old. A little wooden signpost pointed to various paths in the woods where guests could take a stroll. He wiped his glasses clean on the end of his shirt before having a look around. His dad beeped the car horn and gestured at him to hurry up.

He didn't need to climb the steps that led to the front door of the hotel to see the sign that hung on the ornate door knocker. His cousin was right. Closed.

Pity. It would have been good to stay there for the night. There were probably lots of places where he could hide from The Brute and read a book or listen to music. At least then the next twenty-four hours would have passed a lot more quickly.

As he turned back towards the car he suddenly felt that something wasn't quite right. If it had been dark or if he had been on his own, Colm would have been more nervous, but even now, at four in the afternoon, with the sun still in the sky and his parents no more than ten yards away, he didn't feel completely safe.

Relax, he thought, it's just your imagination. But even as the words ran through his head he felt that someone was watching him. He spun around, but there wasn't anybody there. He peered into the woods. It was dark in there and he couldn't see much of anything. For a moment he thought he heard something move in the undergrowth – a cracking twig, the rustling of leaves – but then his father beeped the car horn again and the spell was broken. As quickly as it had arrived, the feeling left him.

'Well?' his father asked through the rolled-down window.

'It's closed,' Colm replied.

'Right. Get in. Let's not waste any more time here.'

Colm climbed into the car. The Brute had stolen even more of the back seat in the couple of minutes he'd been gone, so that when he closed the door the window-winder dug into his side leaving a little circle of red on his chubby belly.

'Dad?'

'Mmmm?'

'Did you see anything strange?'

'Strange? What do you mean strange?'

'You know when you're out somewhere and you get the feeling someone's watching you. I got that feeling. Like someone was watching us from the woods.'

The Brute threw his eyes up to heaven.

'There's nobody watching us from the woods,' said Colm's father.

He was right. There wasn't anyone watching them from the woods. The person who was watching them was on the third floor of the hotel. He was tall and thin, and he shouldn't have been there.

Two

I f the only things you know about private detectives are from watching television programmes or reading about them in books, then you might think that they lead exciting lives full of car chases and shootouts, of racing after criminals and thugs, of beating people up or getting beaten up. In real life things aren't like that. Most private detective work involves long hours on the internet, making endless amounts of phone calls and sitting in cars waiting to take photos of people doing things they shouldn't be doing. To sum up, it's boring. And for Cedric Murphy, who had been a private detective for fifteen years, it was the way things had always been. He didn't mind that much. It wasn't as good as being a professional soccer player, but better than working with sewage.

But Cedric's life had changed three days ago when he'd received a phone call. If he could go back in time he would never have answered the phone; then again, if he had the ability to go back in time he probably would have gone back with the winning Lotto numbers. Instead here he was in his tiny office shaking like a boy who's accidentally smashed every plate in his mother's best dinner set minutes before her family and friends call around for Sunday dinner.

He glanced at his watch again. It had only been thirty seconds since he'd last checked the time. His client was almost ten minutes late. Maybe he wasn't going to turn up. He felt a wave of relief wash over him. He was off the hook. In the clear. Free as a ...

The intercom buzzed and Cedric Murphy sighed. He knew he was in trouble. His hand shook as he pressed the talk button. The voice that crackled over the intercom was calm and strong.

'I have an appointment.'

This was his last chance to back out. He wondered if he should try climbing through the window, but the window was very small and Cedric Murphy was very large. Too many full Irish breakfasts and Indian takeaways for dinner meant he constantly balanced on the slender tightrope between very fat and obese. He promised himself that if he got out of this alive he'd start eating healthily.

'Come on up,' he said into the speaker.

He heard the soft click as the door below opened, followed

by the quiet footsteps of the man as he climbed the narrow stairs. Murphy tried to compose himself. He didn't want to appear nervous. That would give the man the upper hand. He checked his shirt. Damp patches of sweat beneath the arms. That was a giveaway. Even though it was boiling hot in the cramped office, he put his jacket on to cover up the stains. Why hadn't he ever bought a fan or an air conditioner? He was hotter than an unsheared sheep in Death Valley on a cloudless July afternoon. He gulped down a large glass of water, then pretended to be interested in some papers on his desk as the door creaked open and the rat-faced little man entered the office.

'Mr Murphy?' he asked.

The man's accent was American, his nose Roman, his knuckles tattooed. Murphy stood up, banged his head against the naked light bulb and sent it swinging gently to and fro. He acted as if nothing had happened and extended a hand the man didn't bother shaking.

'Call me Cedric.'

'I'll call you Mr Murphy.'

'Whatever you like,' said Cedric in what he hoped was a casual tone. He felt anything but casual. His heart thumped so loudly he was certain the man could hear it.

'Please sit down, Mr ... I'm sorry, I never got your name.'

The man remained standing. His cold eyes examined

every corner of the small office before they settled on Cedric Murphy.

'If you're as good at your job as they say you are, then you already know my name,' he said, with what passed for a smile.

He was right. Cedric Murphy may have been many things – greedy, a bully, a thief – but he was also the best private investigator in the country. The rat-faced man had called him and told him he had a job for him, one which would pay a fortune, but which required absolute secrecy. Murphy had accepted the job and then he had done what he always did – a background check on the man. It had taken him longer than he had expected to find information on his client and he got the feeling that if the man hadn't wanted him to find anything at all, then he wouldn't have. Still, it hadn't been easy. And what he had found out had made his flesh crawl.

'What can I do for you, Mr … Smith?'

'You know who I work for,' said the man. It was a statement, rather than a question.

Murphy nodded. Sweat dripped from his eyebrows and stung his eyes. He had heard a lot of stories about the man's employer. Everybody in his profession had. The tales had terrified him, and Cedric Murphy wasn't a man who frightened easily.

'Then you know he has high standards,' said the man. He took a crumpled photograph from his coat pocket and dropped it onto the desk.

'My employer wants you to find this man.'

Murphy looked at the photo. Nobody he recognised. The man was smiling. Must have been happier times, he thought. He wondered what the poor eejit had done. Something bad if he had men like this after him.

'I'm going to need more than a photograph if I'm to find him.'

The man picked up a pencil and scribbled something on a piece of paper. He folded the paper in half and placed it in front of Cedric Murphy.

'I presume that is all you need,' he said, as he twirled the pencil between his fingers.

Murphy examined what the man had written.

'That'll be enough. It'll take a few days, maybe a week ...'

'You have twelve hours.'

Cedric attempted a gulp, but his throat was too dry. Instead he made a strange sound that would have embarrassed him in other circumstances.

'That's impossible. How can you ...'

'In twelve hours time I will be expecting a telephone call from you giving me directions to wherever this man is located.'

'And if I haven't found him?'

The rat-faced little man snapped the pencil in two.

'I presume I have made myself clear,' he said, leaning in so closely that Cedric Murphy could smell what he had eaten for lunch.

'Crystal,' he replied.

The man looked at his watch.

'Then I shall talk to you again in eleven hours and fifty-nine minutes.'

The man had barely left the office before Cedric picked up the phone.

'Hey, it's me. We're in trouble.'

'What kind?' said the woman on the other end of the line.

Cedric looked at the broken pencil and rubbed the back of his neck.

'The "Oh, look, I'm dead" kind,' he replied.

Three

A black Range Rover blocked their path. Colm's father had driven halfway down the long access path that led from the Red House Hotel to the main road and had come to a stop when the jeep came rumbling towards them from the other direction. Now, the two vehicles were at a standstill, nose to nose. There wasn't enough space for either one of them to pass the other.

'Beep the horn, Joe,' said Colm's mother.

'What good will that do?' his father asked. He was spineless when it came to any sort of confrontation.

'You have the right of way. He's the one who should back up.'

But the driver of the jeep wasn't a man, it was a tiny old woman. And she didn't back up. Instead, she hopped out of the jeep and scuttled over to them.

'How're ye lads?' she asked in a raspy voice that suggested she smoked at least forty cigarettes a day. Her face was criss-crossed with so many wrinkles that if you were bored you could have passed the time playing a game of Xs and Os on her paper-thin skin.

'We're grand,' said Colm's father. 'Look, we were on the road first, so I think you should be the one to back up. If that's OK with you.'

'Sure, that's no problem at all. Do ye not like the hotel?'

'It's closed,' he said to the woman.

'What's that?'

'The hotel's closed,' he shouted, thinking she must be hard of hearing.

'I'm not deaf,' said the old woman. 'I was just surprised at your foolishness. The hotel isn't closed.'

'Well, the sign on the door says it is.'

'Marie,' said the old woman, more to herself than anyone else.

'I'm the owner,' she added. 'I was away for the night and I left my daughter in charge. She must have put the sign up. She'll regret doing that.'

'So, you're not closed?' asked Colm's mother.

'Not at all. Are you looking for rooms?'

Say no, Colm thought without quite knowing why.

'Yes,' said his mother.

The old woman introduced herself as Nellie McMahon ('but ye can call me Mrs McMahon') and within two minutes they were all standing in the reception area of the hotel.

While his parents filled out the check-in forms, Mrs McMahon filled them in on what she had been up to, even though no one had asked her.

'My daughter, she fusses too much. She's like a mother hen, that one. She said that I should take a few days off from the hotel, that I was working too hard, but sure, isn't that what God put us on this earth for – to work hard?'

Colm's attention began to wander. There was something about the old woman's voice that made him want to throw himself through a window to avoid having to listen to another word she said. He looked around the lobby. The furniture was either antique or else it was just very, very old. He wasn't sure what the difference was. Every space on the walls was filled with a painting of an old man or woman who, judging by their clothes, had died a very long time ago.

'She booked me on a three-day break, a bus tour to Knock with a bunch of pensioners,' Mrs McMahon continued.

'Was it good?' Colm's mother asked out of politeness.

'Terrible. Absolutely terrible. They were the greatest shower of bores and moaners I've ever had the misfortune to meet. 'Twas all "me poor leg" this, "me aching back" that. And if they weren't moaning, they were showing me photos of their fat, spoiled grandchildren. I ask you, is there anything more boring than other people's photos?'

'Your stories,' said The Brute, although he said it very quietly.

One of the paintings grabbed Colm's attention. It was a portrait of a young man with long, dark hair and a scar that ran from the corner of his right eye to his upper lip. Unlike the subjects of the other paintings who either smiled proudly showing yellow, stained teeth or looked bored to the point of sleep or death, the young man seemed filled with passion and anger, as if at any moment he would rip free from the canvas and burst into life. But what Colm noticed most of all was his eyes. Blood red.

'And then they'd pass around soggy ham sandwiches and flasks of lukewarm tea. I snuck off the bus in Kilmacorney, thumbed a lift to the station and drove back here. I'll tell ye one thing – I'll never go away with a bunch of auld ones ever again. Boring people are a curse. Isn't that right, Conor?'

Colm looked at her. 'Sorry?'

'It's Colm, not Conor,' corrected his mother.

'You're not boring, are you, Conor? Most of the people you'll meet in life will be boring and they'll hate you if you're interesting. They'll try to change you, but don't let them, Conor, don't let them,' said Mrs McMahon.

'Too late for that. He's already boring. All he does is read books and sleep,' said The Brute.

His aunt gave him an angry look which he expertly ignored.

'Are you a reader?' Mrs McMahon asked Colm.

'He's always got his head stuck in a book,' said Colm's mother.

Mrs McMahon pointed a stubby finger in the direction of a door to the left of the wooden staircase. 'Go in there then. That room has books you never dreamed existed. Your parents can give you a shout when they've settled into their room,' she said.

'You go on as well, Michael,' said Colm's mother.

'I'm going to have a heart attack with the excitement,' said The Brute.

But he followed Colm into the library. Just as he'd thought, it was everything he hated. Books from floor to ceiling. Cracked leather armchairs where boring old people, long since dead, must once have sat reading by a crackling fire on a cold winter's night. The saps.

The smell of must hung in the air as if the room had not been used for a long time. The Brute could see why. What it needed was a forty-two-inch plasma TV, a mini-fridge and a few large bowls filled with crisps and dry-roasted peanuts. If the old woman did that and got Sky on the television it might actually be an OK place to hang out and watch matches. He turned to Colm, about to tell him all this, but when he saw him staring at the books it just bugged him. There was something about his cousin that bugged him no matter what mood he was in, so instead of telling him his idea he found himself saying, 'Remind me, Fishbreath, have I given you your daily dig yet?'

He towered over Colm. His knuckles cracked as he formed a fist.

'You gave me extra digs for the last few days because you were supposed to be going back home today. So you don't owe me any,' Colm said, all his words running together in a panic.

The Brute's face screwed up into an ugly mug of concentration. It didn't take much to confuse him and Colm knew that this was the time to make him forget about the daily dig. He'd remember it later, but Colm always preferred being punched later to being punched now.

'I think there's something not quite right about this place,' Colm said.

'Yeah. The coffin dodger who owns it is as mad as a bag of cats,' said The Brute.

'No, well, yeah, she probably is, but it's not that it's ...'

'You're boring me now. Shut up.'

The Brute slumped into an armchair, plonked his feet on

a highly polished coffee table and began to wiggle his little finger in his ear, pausing from time to time to examine the clumps of wax he extracted.

Colm turned to the books on the mahogany shelves. The old woman was right. It was a strange collection. He'd read a lot of books in his short life, but not one of these. He ran his fingers along the spines of the novels, pausing briefly to read the names of the authors. He only recognised one in every ten. And even those were authors his mother wouldn't allow him to read ('not until you're fourteen, Colm'). Poe. De Maupassant. Sheridan. All leather-bound hardbacks, except one. One that looked completely out of place, even in this unusual library.

'I don't get it. How can you stand being in a room like this? It's so ... depressing,' said The Brute as he wondered whether or not to sample a juicy portion of ear wax.

Colm didn't hear him. There was something very different about that book. He wasn't sure what it was, but there was definitely something. All the other books looked clean and neat and well cared for, but this one looked as if it hadn't been touched in years, decades even. The writing on the spine was covered with a thick layer of dust.

He was about to reach out and wipe it away when he got a bad feeling. Deep down in the pit of his stomach where all his bad feelings hung out. It was the same one he got when they were picking teams for soccer at lunchtime and he knew he was going to be the last one picked. The feeling he got when the teacher asked him a question and he didn't know the answer. The sort of feeling that said, whatever else you do, do not even think for one second about touching this book. The kind of feeling that shouldn't be ignored.

'What's wrong with you?' The Brute asked.

'Nothing.'

'Then why are you staring at that book?'

It was true. Colm was staring. He couldn't take his eyes off it.

'Stop being such a girl. Take it if you want it.'

Reasons why Michael James McGrath hated The Rancid Reject:

1. He was boring. He never did anything exciting or dangerous. Ever.
2. He couldn't take a punch. And it wasn't like he hit him hard. Even when he gave him an easy knuckler, the little weasel would look up at him like a hurt puppy. Sometimes he looked like he was going to cry.
3. He was scared to do anything without checking with his mam or dad if it was OK or not. He always did the right thing. The eejit.

4. Most importantly, Colm had a way of always making him feel thick. Sometimes it was the way he said something, like when he used a big word in a sentence, other times it was just the way he looked at him. He didn't know how he did it, but even by just raising an eyebrow he could make him feel like he was the most stupid person on earth.

Colm hesitated, then turned away from the book.

'Hah!' said The Brute.

'What?'

'I knew you wouldn't go near it.'

'I don't want to look at it,' said Colm.

'Right,' he sniffed.

'I don't.'

'You're not going to touch it cos you're scared. You're like a kitten – always scared.'

'I'm not scared,' said Colm, but even he knew he was protesting a bit too much.

'You are. You're a Grade A coward. A chicken.'

The Brute began to make clucking noises and flapped his arms like a chicken. It wasn't a pretty sight, but it was enough to rile Colm.

'Right. I'll prove I'm not a chicken. I'm going to take it off the shelf.'

He stood in front of the book. Still hesitating. The Brute switched from clucking to squawking. Colm felt the anger building inside him. He could hear the blood rushing in his ears. He'd have given anything to punch his cousin on his fat nose, just to shut him up. He was the most annoying person he'd ever met.

The Brute stopped squawking. 'I knew you wouldn't do it.'

But he was wrong. Without waiting another second Colm wiped the dust away until he could read the title.

The Book of Dread.

'Don't touch it!' a girl squealed.

The next thing Colm heard was a bang as The Brute's feet slid across the coffee table and he fell off the armchair with a tremendous thump and a muffled swear word. He tried to stand up, but failed. His legs had somehow knotted themselves around each other. After a few seconds he managed to untie himself and popped back up, acting like nothing had happened, even though his face was bright red.

'I meant to do that,' he lied.

The girl stood at the door.

'Sorry guys, I didn't mean to frighten you,' she said in an American accent.

'My gran said you were here and I came in to say hello.

When I saw you reaching for … well, I just didn't want you to touch that book.'

'I wasn't going to,' Colm said. Another lie.

'Yeah, I'm sure you weren't.'

They looked at each other for a few moments until Colm began to feel awkward. He often felt like that when he met someone new and couldn't really think of what to say to them. The girl smiled. It was a warm, friendly smile, a smile that made him relax. He found his voice.

'Hi. I'm Colm,' he said. Not very witty or entertaining, but better than silence.

'Hey. Lauryn,' said the girl.

They both looked at The Brute and waited for him to say something, but he didn't speak. He tried, but it just didn't work out for him. His mouth opened and formed an O so that he looked like a particularly large and gormless goldfish. Then his face, which had only just returned to its usual colour, turned red again. Starting at his neck, the wave of crimson slowly crept up his face until it reached the tips of his ears. And then, finally, after what seemed like hours, a word.

'Heeeuurrghh.'

Obviously not an English word, but possibly in some language. Either way, as introductions go it wasn't the best. Colm came to the rescue.

'That's my cousin, The ... Michael. He's having trouble speaking because he just fell off the chair. Probably banged his head or something.'

'Jeeuuuugghh,' said The Brute. What he was trying to say was that the fall wasn't the reason for his sudden inability to form words and sentences. It was Lauryn. She was tall, blonde and no more than fourteen years old. And even though he didn't know that much about girls, Colm could see that she was beautiful. 'TV beautiful' was how The Brute would describe her later when he was able to speak more clearly. He meant that she wasn't just pretty like the girl who lived next door or the girl who sat beside you in school. She was a stunner.

Silence again.

'Em,' said Colm. 'The book. Did you not want me to touch it cos it's worth a lot of money or something?'

'Huh? Oh, I couldn't tell you. It might be, but I don't care about that,' said Lauryn.

'What is it then?'

'It's cursed.'

'Cursed?'

'Yeah, but that doesn't really matter, cos you didn't touch it,' she said.

Colm felt an icy chill run down his back. Cursed. He didn't like the sound of that. Not one little bit.

'Yeah, that was lucky,' he said. He waited until the girl looked away, then stuffed his hands into his pockets to hide his dusty fingers.

'It's a bad curse. I mean, I know all curses are bad, but this one's a real kicker,' Lauryn said. She took out a packet of gum and offered it around. The Brute shook his head.

'This curse, what does it do?' Colm asked, trying to sound like he hadn't a care in the world.

'Whoever touches the book is supposed to die within a day,' Lauryn said.

The Brute found his voice again.

'Cool,' he said.

·◆·

The Book of Dread (1)

February 29th, 1896

Today I journeyed south. It was an unpleasant experience. On the train I was hemmed into my seat by the most boorish man I ever had the misfortune to meet. He was fat and smelled of beer and turnips and every ten minutes he broke wind (with no sense of shame; the scoundrel even laughed).

The train only took me to within ten miles of my destination. From there the only transport I could find was carriage by an uncovered horse and trap. Naturally, it rained and all of my belongings were soaked through. I wished I had not been so hasty in accepting the offer of employment given to me by my uncle, the esteemed R.B. Stowely. I had been proud that he had entrusted the job to me, yet when the horse clip-clopped over the unpaved road making me sick (and causing the loss of at least one of my leather satchels) I heartily wished I was back in my comfortable home in Dublin rather than the wretched countryside. I was in a dark mood.

All that changed when I saw the Red House. It is a magnificent estate nestled in the countryside, a stone's throw from a river and surrounded on three sides by a large forest. There is a strong smell of pine in the air.

It won't be easy to transform this place from a wealthy family home into a hotel, but I shall succeed.

Four

Cedric Murphy sat in his car, thinking. Thinking and eating a fat, greasy breakfast roll, but mostly thinking. He had eleven hours to find the man in the photograph. The one thing he didn't think about was what would happen to him if he failed to find the man. He definitely didn't want to think about that.

His assistant climbed into the car. Her name was Kate Finkle and she wasn't pleasing to the eye. She wasn't pleasing to the ear either. Her voice was a shrill, grating thing that could make even the most beautiful poetry seem like torture, but none of that mattered to Cedric. He liked her. Kate was his only friend in the world.

She lived in a tiny council flat with three cats, two gold-fish and a broken doorbell. She worked three days a week for Cedric and the days she spent in the office were the only time she truly felt happy.

They usually communicated by being mean to each other. They both enjoyed this. Some people are like that.

'This is exciting,' Kate said, lighting up a fat cigar.

'No smoking in the car,' Cedric said. He added a cough for effect, but she ignored him and continued to puff away. Cedric started up the car, drove out in front of a lorry and made a rude gesture when the lorry driver beeped his horn.

'Wait a second. What do you mean exciting? My potential death is exciting to you?'

'That's not what I meant. Usually we're stuck in the office, looking up financial records or addresses, maybe putting in a few phone calls to get some information for someone who wants to check up on an employee, but this, this is different. It's life or death. It's the open road. It's adventure. It's not boring is what I'm saying.'

'Boring is good. Boring pays the bills. Give me boring any day of the week.'

'Come on, Ced. You know what I mean.'

She was the only person who called him Ced. Only two others had ever tried and both of them had ended up in hospital. He had never tried to stop Kate calling him Ced. He liked it.

'You don't know this guy. Him picking me for this job, well, it was a boot load of really bad luck for us.'

Cedric put his foot down on the accelerator. He was a reckless driver and he pushed the Ford Focus as close to the edge as was possible. He'd have preferred to drive a really fast car – something flashy like a Lamborghini – but he imagined that it would be difficult to engage in undercover work in a yellow Italian sports car. They sort of stood out.

'So, tell me about the bad guy.'

'They call him The Ghost,' said Cedric Murphy.

'Why?'

'Because when someone came up with the nickname The Phantom, most of his gang didn't know what a phantom was. They're not the brightest.'

Kate arched an eyebrow. This meant he hadn't answered her question and she wanted an answer. Now. Cedric understood. They got each other that way.

'The Ghost? Right. It's because no one's ever seen him. He's the head of one of the biggest criminal organisations in the world and none of the people working for him have even met him.'

'How does he get anything done?'

'Telephone calls. The internet. Mail drops. Leaves cash out for employees. Notes telling them where to be, what to rob, how to do it and so on.'

'But how does he stop them stealing from him? If he never sees them how does he know what they're up to?'

'That's the good part. He *always* knows what they're up to. Nobody has figured out how, but he does. One time, one of the gang tried to rip him off. Stole a small amount, fifty thousand dollars, something like that.'

Kate whistled. 'Fifty thousand is a small amount?'

'Not to you or me. But to him it's like change you'd find down the back of your couch, stuck between cat hairs and a melted bar of chocolate. Anyway, the story goes that he wasn't that bothered about the money. Like I said, it was a small amount for him, but he couldn't have anyone steal from him and think he'd get away with it. Next thing you know, all of the gang would be at it, fifty thousand here, half a million there. He couldn't allow that to happen.'

'I get it,' Kate said. 'He killed him to make a point. To show the others what would happen if they stole from him.'

'No.'

'No?'

'The thief disappeared. The others in the gang thought he'd just gone on the run, but then his family disappeared, and his relations and his wife's relations. Twenty-eight people disappeared in six weeks. Just like that,' said Cedric with a click of his fingers.

Kate let the thought sink in. Suddenly this didn't seem like much of an adventure anymore.

'They were never seen again,' he added. This last remark was unnecessary.

'And no one has any idea who The Ghost is?'

'No. There's gossip, but nothing concrete. They say he moves around. From city to city, town to town. If he thinks someone even suspects who he is, he moves. No hesitation. He has no family. No friends. No ties.'

'He must be lonely,' Kate said. She stubbed out her cigar in the car's ashtray.

'Yeah. That's what I'm worried about. The world's most dangerous criminal is lonely. Boo hoo.'

'I was just saying.'

'Well don't,' Cedric snapped. He apologised immediately.

'It's okay. You're just a bit stressed,' she said.

'Just a bit,' he agreed.

They drove in silence for a while.

'So who are we looking for?'

Cedric leaned across her and grabbed the photo from the glove compartment. He took his eyes off the road for a moment and the car lurched onto the footpath. A surly teenager who was slouching along the path with his hands stuffed into his hoodie pockets suddenly came alive, shrieked and leaped into an old man's garden to avoid being mangled. Cedric swerved back onto the road. Kate watched in the wing mirror as the teenager reappeared on the footpath hotly pursued by the old man's German Shepherd.

She turned her gaze back to the photo.

'You don't know him, I suppose?' Cedric asked.

'The man in the photo? Never saw him before in my life.'

'It was a long shot.'

'Is that all we have to go on?' she asked.

Cedric nodded. 'Oh, wait. There's a note. Hold the wheel.'

Kate steered the car while Cedric rummaged around his jacket pockets until he found the piece of paper. He handed it to Kate and retook the steering wheel.

'The Lazarus Key,' she read. 'What does that mean?'

'I didn't know either so I googled it.'

'You googled it? Top notch detective work there, Ced.'

'Thanks.'

'So what is it?' she asked.

'Oh, just some magic mumbo-jumbo. Bit of nonsense really, like that astronomy you're into.'

'You know it's astrology. You're just trying to wind me up,' she said.

He was. It usually worked too.

'I'm not going to fall for it this time,' Kate added.

Cedric waited. Any minute now.

'Astrology is a real science, you know.'

'Kate, astrology is about as real as the rubies in your earrings.'

'You can hardly expect me to wear real rubies on the wages you pay. So what did you find out about this Lazarus Key?'

'Bits and pieces. I don't think it's going to help us. Something about a secret society in the US in the 1800s. Nasty beggars it seems. They believed the Key gave them some sort of eternal life, but it was stolen from them by some English guy and never seen again.'

'Eternal life? Right. Lazarus. Like in the bible. The man who came back from the dead,' Kate said.

'Yep. I presume that's it. Probably just some scary story to frighten the kids. No truth to it,' he said. 'There was even a tattoo they all used to have on the inside of their arms. A skull inside a diamond shape. I copied it on the back of the page.'

Kate flipped the page over. Just like he'd described it. 'Pleasant lads, aren't they?' she said with a shudder.

The picture made her uncomfortable. The people she usually came across in her line of work were ones who faked an injury after an accident at work and then were spotted dancing in a nightclub when they were supposed to be tucked up in bed with a bad back. This secret

society sounded dangerous. 'You think this Ghost is after the Lazarus thingy?'

'Key. Yeah, but not for its supposed life-giving properties. It's probably worth a fortune. Guys like him are only interested in one thing and that's money,' he said.

Cedric took a left turn and soon they were surrounded by cars filled with impatient drivers who beeped the horns, flashed the lights and looked angry, stressed and on the verge of tears, all at the same time. They were on the M50, Dublin's ring road. From here they could take the main road to anywhere in Ireland. Cedric eased the car into the fast lane which was moving so slowly that Colm's father wouldn't have felt uncomfortable driving there.

'What's the plan, Ced?'

'The man we're looking for is American and two days ago he was still in America. If he came to Ireland in the last forty-eight hours he had to pass through a port or airport.'

'Unless he was smuggled in,' Kate added.

Cedric's shoulders slumped. 'If he was smuggled in then we haven't a hope of finding him,' he said.

Kate gave him a moment to feel sorry for himself. 'So what did you do?'

'I called a few friends at the airport and ports. Faxed them a copy of the photo. Promised them a big reward if they found him on CCTV.'

'If they were real friends you wouldn't have to pay them a reward.'

'If I was relying on your friends then the only ones I could show the photo to would be a bunch of cats.'

'Don't forget the goldfish,' Kate said.

Cedric smiled. That was more like it. Being mean to each other. But the smile didn't last for long. Relying on his friends – OK contacts – in the airports and ports was as much a long shot as Kate knowing the man in the photo. Two days of CCTV footage meant looking at thousands and thousands of people and hoping someone looked at the camera at just the right time so that they could be recognised. And what if the man was wearing a disguise? The chances of finding his target were as likely as finding a lost contact lens in a swimming pool. But then Cedric's mobile rang and he had his first and last bit of good luck.

·◆·

The Book of Dread (2)

March 14th, 1896

The last fortnight has not been easy. The work has been hard – knocking down walls, landscaping the overgrown gardens – but that is not what concerns me. I expected no less. What troubles me is the men I have hired from the local village. They are not bad fellows and they toil well enough, but they are not happy here. At first I thought it was that they did not like me. Occasionally I have heard them snigger as I passed – at my dandyish clothing and my Dublin ways – but it is more than that. There are certain areas of the estate where they refuse to venture. They mutter darkly about ghosts and ghouls and things that go bump in the night. They whisper of strange visions and more than once I have heard mention of a mysterious Key, but they stopped talking whenever they saw that I was listening.

Finally, my patience grew thin and I cornered one fellow – a skinny, miserable wretch who goes by the name of Mahony. He explained to me that the villagers do not like this place. They believe that something evil lurks here. I cannot abide such superstitious nonsense and I was sorely tempted to give him a good beating to knock some sense into him. Instead, I told him to carry on with his work – which was to thin out some of the forest so that there will be walking paths for the guests – but he begged me not to force him to undertake the task. He didn't want to go into the woods. He was terrified! I told him that if he didn't then he would be unemployed by the day's end. He had no choice but to do the work as he has a wife and nine children to support. He went off in glum spirits.

Five

Colm wondered if being cursed was ever a good thing. Probably not. The American girl had said that anybody who touched the book was dead by the morning. Dead definitely wasn't good. He liked being alive. Sure, there were plenty of annoying things in his life – homework, getting up early on winter mornings when the heating was broken, boiled cabbage; but there was good stuff too – lying in bed reading a book when everyone else in the house was asleep, DVDs, summer holidays.

'Is there a cure for the curse?' Colm asked.

'Not unless they've discovered a cure for death,' Lauryn said.

The Brute laughed long and loud. A little too long and too loud.

She frowned. 'Is he all right?'

'He's fine. I think he's just happy to be here,' Colm replied.

'Weird. Why are you so worried about the curse anyway? You didn't touch the book, did you?'

'Me? No. Definitely not. But supposing someone did, then is there some, you know, way to stop it?'

Before Lauryn had a chance to answer Mrs McMahon barrelled into the library. She had a portable phone clamped to her ear and was in the middle of a conversation.

'I don't care who gave you the day off, Brendan. I'm your boss and if you're not at work in an hour, don't bother turning up tomorrow,' she said into the phone. She hung up. 'I see you've met my granddaughter. I hope you were polite enough to introduce yourself to the lads, Lauryn.'

'You bet, Grandma.'

'Don't call me Grandma. You know I hate it.'

'Sorry, Grandma.'

Mrs McMahon gave her a look that would have terrified a rampaging bull, but it didn't appear to bother Lauryn in the slightest.

'What's wrong with you, Conor? You're white as a sheet,' Mrs McMahon said.

'Car sick,' Lauryn replied.

'Good for you,' said Mrs McMahon, who wasn't really listening. 'Where's your mother, Lauryn? I need to have a word with her.'

'She's gone for a walk, I think.'

'A walk? The useless article. Do you know why she closed the hotel? Was it too much work for her to run it for a night or two?'

'No, it was rats,' Lauryn said.

'Rats? What do you mean by rats?'

'She saw a rat in one of the rooms. A huge guy. As big as a cat or a small dog. It had cruel black eyes and a mean look on its face. She said you couldn't have guests staying in a hotel that had been taken over by rats.'

Mrs McMahon couldn't have been more offended if you put her in a suit and called her Bob.

'There are no rats in this hotel,' she thundered.

'Er, Gran, maybe you should keep your voice down. Anyway, there's no need to worry. There's an exterminator due here any minute.'

'An exterminator! I'll exterminate her. Rats. I never heard the likes of it. This hotel has won seven hygiene awards and I go away for one night and a rat turns up.'

She must have forgotten about Colm and The Brute because suddenly she turned to them and smiled her biggest smile. It wasn't a pleasant sight.

'Now lads, you'll have to forgive my daughter and her wild imagination. She's been in America for twenty years and she's a bit flighty. She probably thought she saw a rat, but I guarantee you she didn't. Anyway, two big strong lads like you aren't scared of a harmless little rodent are you?'

'No way,' said The Brute. He puffed out his chest. It gave him the appearance of a preening gorilla.

'My mam hates rats. She says they carry loads of diseases,' Colm said.

'Creep,' muttered The Brute under his breath.

'Nonsense,' said Mrs McMahon. 'Rats get a bad press, but they're cute auld things really. All that stuff about diseases is just an exaggeration. Sure, what disease could a furry little rat carry anyway?'

'Rabies,' said Lauryn.

'Bubonic plague,' said Colm.

'Weil's disease,' said Lauryn.

'OK, I get the point. Anyway, the rat, if he exists at all …' said Mrs McMahon glaring at Lauryn, 'will soon be an ex-rat, so your parents don't have to find out, do they?'

She winked at The Brute.

'Rats? Never heard anyone say anything about a rat,' he said, playing along. He shot Colm a filthy look. It meant keep your mouth shut. Colm did.

'That's the spirit,' said Mrs McMahon. She seemed impressed with The Brute. 'It'll be our little secret.'

'Your secret's safe with us, Mrs McMahon. And if I see

the rat I'll kill it for you. With my bare hands. It's nothing to be worried about,' he said in a fawning manner.

'Good man, Michael. That's what I like to hear. I wish more of the young lads these days showed your sort of fortitude.'

The Brute didn't know what fortitude meant, but he thought it was a compliment. Colm wondered what was wrong with his cousin. Why was he being so nice? It was strange. He was used to him being horrible and he was a lot more comfortable with that.

The phone rang and Mrs McMahon answered it immediately.

'Stephen. It's about time you got back to me. I must have left half a dozen messages. Work. One hour. Don't even think about being late.'

She hung up and handed The Brute a key. Unlike most hotels where you use a plastic key card to get into your room, this was an old-fashioned metal key with a leather tag clipped to the key ring. The number thirteen was stamped on the tag in big black numerals.

'I hope you're not superstitious. Your parents have gone in to the restaurant for a complimentary cup of tea while I check their room is ready.' She turned to her granddaughter. 'Lauryn, did you even think of offering the lads something to drink?'

'Sorry, I forgot,' Lauryn said.

'Forgot's not good enough. Now lads, if ye need anything, anything at all, just ask.'

The phone rang for a third time and Mrs McMahon disappeared into the lobby. Lauryn closed the door after her, but they could still hear her shouting into the phone.

'Her bark is worse than her bite,' said Lauryn. 'She's actually kinda cool.'

'If you like scary people,' said Colm.

Lauryn laughed at that, even though Colm hadn't realised he'd said something funny.

'Where are you guys from?'

The Brute had gone silent again, so Colm answered. 'I'm from Dublin and Michael's from Baile Eilís.'

'Baile Eilís? That's not far from here, right?'

'No. Not too far,' Colm said. He had grown tired of the polite conversation. He wanted to know more about the curse and his impending doom.

'You're American,' The Brute blurted out in a voice that was far too loud. Colm wondered what was wrong with him. He was acting very strangely again now that Mrs McMahon had left.

'Yep. Philadelphia born and bred. Go Eagles.'

'But your grandmother's Irish,' he said in a slightly more normal voice.

'Is he always this sharp?' Lauryn asked.

Colm figured she was being sarcastic so he didn't bother answering.

'My mom grew up here, but she went to the US when she was twenty. She was only going to stay a few years, but then she met my dad and they got married so she didn't came back to Ireland, not even after they split up. I don't think my gran's ever forgiven her for that.'

'Lauryn, can I ask you something?'

'Sure, kid.'

Colm didn't like being called a kid, but he didn't know how to stop her from saying it without being rude, so he didn't mention it.

'This curse. Can you tell me a bit more about it?'

'Wow, you're really interested in the curse, aren't you? That's the third time you've mentioned it. It's a long story,' she said.

Colm waited for her to tell the story, but she didn't. Instead she just popped another piece of gum into her mouth.

Three thoughts went through The Brute's head at once, which was two more than usual. He was acting like an eejit in front of the most beautiful girl he had ever seen. He'd probably got away with it so far, he thought, but he needed to make a good impression. Fast. His dad had always told him to act confident even when his insides were churning. Cool and confident. That was the key.

He sat back in the armchair and swung his legs on to the table, more carefully this time. 'Hey, Lauryn. Tell the kid that story if you want. We've got all the time in the world, babe.' In his defence, it sounded a lot better in his head than it did when the words were out there in the real world.

'Two things,' said Lauryn. 'One – take your feet off the table right this second.'

The Brute's feet were back on the ground before Lauryn had even finished the sentence.

'And two – if you ever call me "babe" again, I'll thump you so hard you'll forget your own name. Are we clear?'

'Yes,' said The Brute. He looked so upset that for a moment Colm thought he was going to cry. The girl was pretty, but she was also like her grandmother. Frightening.

'I've gotta go check something. Catch you guys later,' she said.

Neither of them were happy to see her leave, but for very different reasons.

·◆·

The Book of Dread (3)

March 15th, 1896

Mahony has disappeared. No one knows what has happened to him. He was working in the forest all day and his fellow labourers presumed he had returned home by himself when they didn't see him at day's end. It was only when his wife raised the alarm the next morning that anyone realised he was missing. We spent the day searching the woods, but there was no trace of him to be found. I think he must have met with some kind of accident, but there are grumblings from the workers that there was something other than mere fate at play. They have downed tools and are refusing to work here anymore. They say that it is this place, this curse of the Red House that has claimed him. Without them, I shall not be able to open the hotel on time. I am ruined.

March 26th, 1896

Mahony is still missing. I have been working on my own for the last ten days. The villagers refuse to help me even though I promised to triple their wages. They are too frightened to even set foot on the grounds of the Red House. Their weakness of character sickens me.

It was eleven o'clock when I finished my day's labour. I was exhausted and wanted nothing more than to take to my bed, but I forced myself to walk to the village. I had not seen another human being in five days and was desperate for conversation even if the only people I could talk to were simpletons. I went to one of the many public houses and consumed ale with the only man who would talk to me. When he was drunk he told me a very interesting story about the mysterious thing the men mentioned. It is called the Lazarus Key. If his story is true and not just some drunken rambling I could make my fortune. I will return to Dublin in the morning to undertake research.

Six

The argument had been raging downstairs for thirty-four seconds when Colm decided to lie on the floor of the hotel bedroom and press his left ear to the ground. Words floated up from below, words like 'close the hotel ... ruin me ... how dare you'.

One of the voices belonged to Mrs McMahon. Colm was sure of it. The other voice was quieter, not as raspy and he didn't recognise it. Probably her daughter, he thought. What was her name? Marie, wasn't it? Mrs McMahon said something that Colm couldn't quite make out. All he knew was that she was winning the argument, or maybe she was just shouting the loudest.

He needed a glass. In films when someone wanted to hear something in another room they always pressed the open part of the glass to the wall and their ear to the other end. He wondered if that would work with floors. But then he realised that the only glasses were in the bathroom where The Brute had been for the last twenty minutes, taking a shower if the constant sound of running water was anything to go by.

Colm had tried to his best not to think about the curse. He'd done anything he could to distract himself. He'd tried to read his book, but he couldn't concentrate. The words just blurred together until they were one big unreadable blob.

Then he'd explored the room. It didn't take long. It was a nice enough room, he supposed, if you ignored the hideous pink curtains and the lace trimmings that were draped over every available flat surface. Mrs McMahon really seemed to like lace.

He'd opened and closed every drawer he could find, but there wasn't much of interest there – a few extra bed sheets and some headed notepaper with the words *Red House Hotel* embossed in red (of course) at the top of the page.

Then he'd spent ten minutes staring out the window at the tree-tops down below and he'd found that if you bounced high enough on the bed that you could see a river on the far side of the trees, just where they began to thin out. It wasn't a bad view, if you liked that sort of thing. From Colm's bedroom window at home all you could see were a

Spar shop and traffic lights. Sometimes if he hadn't a new book to read or if there was nothing good on television, he'd sit at the window and watch the hoodies hassle the people going in and out of the shop.

Finally, he'd gone to number fifteen, the room where his parents were staying, and tried to talk to his father, but he was in a foul mood. He'd said that some of the hotel staff had returned and he'd made the mistake of letting a porter carry his bags up to his room. When the man had stood by the door his father had realised he wanted a tip, but he'd had nothing smaller than a twenty euro note on him and when he gave it to the porter – who smelled of fish – he hadn't even given him any change!

'Twenty euro to carry a couple of bags up two flights of stairs. Can you imagine that? The world's gone mad,' he'd said. 'And what makes it worse is he didn't even smile. He looked like he'd rather be anywhere else in the world than here. He had a moustache too. My mother, your grand-mother, told me you could never trust a man who wore a moustache. And you know what – she was right.'

Colm had noticed that a small vein in his father's forehead had begun to throb. This meant he was seriously angry. It was a step up from his bald patch turning red, so he'd changed the subject and told him what Lauryn had said, but his father hadn't seemed that interested, and when he'd started reading his newspaper Colm took this as a sign that he should go back to his own room. When he'd got there he'd heard the raised voices coming from downstairs.

The bathroom door opened and The Brute emerged.

'What are you doing on the floor, you mope?'

There was something different about his cousin. For one thing he'd called him a mope. This was one of the mildest insults in his arsenal. And for another, he was clean. That was odd. Also, he seemed to be wearing a new shirt and his hair was slicked back.

And then the smell hit him. Colm almost gagged.

'What's that stink?' he spluttered. He rushed to the open window and breathed in some fresh, clean air.

'What are you on about?' said The Brute, but he looked embarrassed.

'Is it aftershave?' Colm asked between gasps of air.

'What's it to you if it is?'

It *was* aftershave. And it wasn't like he'd just dabbed on a little bit behind the ears, like Colm's mother always made his father do when they were going on a night out. Judging by the smell it was as if The Brute had taken a bath in the stuff.

'I didn't know you shaved,' Colm wheezed. The smell seemed to have taken up permanent residence in his nasal passages and he could taste it at the back of the throat. It was vile.

'You're just jealous cos you don't shave.'

'Of course I don't. I'm only eleven.'

He had no answer for that.

'Why were you on the floor?' he asked, changing the subject.

'There was a fight going on downstairs. I was trying to listen to it.'

Suddenly The Brute was interested.

'A fight. Excellent.' He threw a few shadow punches.

'No, not that sort of fight. An argument. I think it was Mrs McMahon and her daughter.'

'Two old dears arguing. And you were interested? You're such an eejit.'

Colm bit back a sarcastic reply. Be nice, he thought. Just make polite conversation. This will soon be over. You'll either be back in Dublin or dead.

'You can see a river if you jump on the bed,' he said, just for something to say.

'Who cares? Stop being such a girl,' said The Brute. He put on a girlish voice. 'Oh, look at the water. It takes my breath away. It's so beautiful I could almost weep tears of joy.'

There was a knock at the door.

'It's your mother. You answer it,' said The Brute.

'She never knocks,' said Colm. It was true. She never did.

It was one of the few things about her that annoyed him. That and the fact that she always tidied his room. He hated it when she did that.

He answered the door. It was Lauryn.

'Hey kid,' she said taking a well-chewed piece of gum from her mouth and dropping it into his hand. 'It's lost its flavour. Get rid of it for me, would ya.'

Colm didn't really like being bossed around by someone who was a virtual stranger, but he wanted to stay on Lauryn's good side. She knew about the curse after all and she might be able to help him out later on. He took the gum and threw it into the metal bin beneath the dresser.

'Hey Michael,' she said.

'All right?' said The Brute in a voice that was much deeper than his normal voice. He smiled. It didn't work out right. As if smiling was a skill he had only recently learned.

'I just wanted to say sorry. About earlier. I was a bit crabby. I have a lot on my ...' Lauryn began, but then her nose wrinkled in disgust. 'Phew, what's that awful stench?'

'Colm was trying on some of his dad's aftershave.' The Brute said. 'And he doesn't even shave,' he added un-necessarily.

'Why would you do that, Colm? Wow, it really is awful. Your dad has the worst taste in aftershave.'

'He sure does,' agreed The Brute.

'I don't know what I was thinking,' Colm said. He didn't know why he was lying for The Brute, but he was too tired to argue.

Lauryn sat down in the armchair by the window. 'That's why I called up. Just to say sorry. What are you guys up to?'

'Just chilling,' said The Brute. He tried to make himself look as cool as possible, but it wasn't easy to look cool while sitting on the edge of a bed with a pink duvet.

Lauryn didn't notice. She seemed distracted, as if there was something else on her mind. Something important that she wanted to say to them, but she wasn't sure how to say it. Instead she just continued to make idle chit-chat.

'Do you like the room? Number thirteen is my favourite room in the hotel,' she said.

'Yeah, it's class. You can even see the river if you jump on the bed,' The Brute said.

'You noticed that? I'm impressed. When we came to visit when I was small I used to love jumping up and down on the bed so I could see the river.'

'Yeah, well Michael's fourteen and he still loves jumping up and down on the bed,' Colm said.

The Brute shot him an angry look. He raised his index finger as if to say that he owed Colm one. Yep, welcome ladies and gentlemen to the Red House Hotel, scene of this evening's punchathon.

Lauryn spotted Colm's book on the dresser and reached across to pick it up. She turned it over so that she could see the cover.

'This is one of my all-time favourites. Which one of you guys is reading this?'

'Me,' lied The Brute. He glared at Colm with the sort of look that said, if you disagree with me I'm going to beat you to a pulp. Colm kept his mouth shut even though he already knew there was a good chance he was going to be beaten to a pulp.

'I know a lot of people say it's not the best book he's written, but I think it's brilliant. Do you read a lot?'

The Brute appeared to give this some thought. 'Do you?'

'Oh, yeah. I always have my head stuck in a book. My mom says that even if the Superbowl was taking place outside my bedroom window, I wouldn't look up from whatever book I was reading.'

'Books are great,' said The Brute. He had started to squirm a bit. He was uncomfortable with the way the conversation was going, but he didn't know how to stop it. It was like a runaway train.

'So what other books do you like?' Lauryn asked.

The Brute looked terrified. If he was honest and said that he never read anything, then Lauryn would *think* he was a fool; if he lied and she asked him some questions about the books he was supposed to have read then she'd *know* he was a fool. Either way, he was bound to lose.

He was saved by the unusual sight of Colm's mother skipping into the room. She had a huge smile on her face, the sort of smile that Colm hadn't seen for a very long time.

'I love this hotel,' she said in a weird sing-song voice. She sounded giddy. And then Colm realised, with a rising feeling of panic, what was going to happen next. He knew by the wild look in her eyes. She was going to hug him. Or kiss him. In front of The Brute and Lauryn.

It was worse than that.

It seemed to happen in slow motion. First she grabbed him in a huge bear hug and held him so tightly his face was squashed right against her chest. Then she planted a big, juicy smacker right on his forehead. A hug *and* a kiss. The double-whammy.

His cheeks burned with embarrassment. Out of the corner of his eye he could see Lauryn and The Brute smirking. Great, now they were thinking that he was a mammy's boy, the worst sort of boy to be. Why did these things always happen to him? He was used to his dad embarrassing him, but now his mam was at it as well. Why were parents so mental? He wished they'd just disappear.

'Isn't it just fantastic to be here?' his mother said. Then

she noticed Lauryn and her voice changed. She sobered up. 'Who's this?'

'Hi, I'm Lauryn,' she said with a confident handshake.

'And who exactly are you?'

'I'm Mrs McMahon's granddaughter, Marie's daughter,' Lauryn said.

'You're American,' said Colm's mother who had a knack for pointing out the obvious.

'Yep. American,' said Lauryn. 'Philly born and bred. Go Eagles.'

It must be a phrase she uses every time she meets someone, Colm thought.

'My husband was telling me you were making up some story about my son being cursed if he touched a book.'

Lauryn began to shift uneasily in her seat.

'It's a legend around here. It's ...'

'I don't care what it is – if you frighten my son, I'll legend you.' She was always issuing threats like that. They never really made sense, but there was something about the way she said them that meant you'd be mad to ignore them.

'You may think because you're a cool teenager you can just make fun of my little Colm, but that's not going to happen. Have I made myself clear?'

'Yes, ma'am,' said Lauryn.

Colm had never really understood what was meant by

the phrase 'I wished the ground would open up and swallow me', but now he did. Perfectly. He would have given anything – his right arm (his left arm, his teeth), all his Sherlock Holmes books, his second-hand X-Box – if the floor had given way and he'd slipped out of sight, never to be seen by any of them again. She'd said 'my little Colm'. Right in front of them. Did she even know what she was doing to him?

She turned to Colm and The Brute. 'Mrs McMahon has been kind enough to get some of the kitchen staff back for the night, even though we're the only guests. We'll meet up in the restaurant in an hour. It's in a room to the right of the reception desk.'

'Yeah, there's a sign on the door. It says "restaurant" in big black letters. It's probably somewhere around there,' said The Brute. He'd gone forty-two minutes without a sarcastic remark. The record had to end sometime.

'Michael ...'

'Sorry, Auntie Mary,' The Brute said before she had the chance to humiliate him.

'Right. You two. One hour.' She looked at her watch. 'That's a quarter-past seven. Don't be late.'

Colm breathed a sigh of relief when she left the room. He hoped nobody would mention what had just happened.

'My little Colm, huh?' Lauryn said.

No such luck.

'Do you want me to give you a huggy-wuggy?' said The Brute.

'Or a kissy-wissy,' said Lauryn with a giggle, although for some reason The Brute looked sort of cross when she said that.

Colm didn't even bother trying to defend himself. What could he say?

'I'd better go,' Lauryn said.

'Sure,' said The Brute.

'See you later, guys,' she said.

The Brute spoke just before she left the room.

'Lauryn, can I ask you something?' he said.

'Shoot,' she replied.

The Brute took this to mean he should go ahead and ask. He cleared his throat. He was building up to something big, but before he said it he turned to Colm.

'You. In the bathroom. Now. This is a private conversation,' he said.

Colm was about to protest, but decided to go along with the demand, just for an easy life. He'd had enough problems today as it was. He went into the bathroom and sat on the edge of the cast iron bath. He could hear the murmur of conversation from outside, but he couldn't make out what they were saying. First the low tones of The Brute, then Lauryn's higher-pitched voice. Finally, he heard the bedroom door close. That must be Lauryn leaving, he thought. He waited for The Brute to tell him it was OK to come out of the bathroom, but when he'd heard nothing after five minutes, he opened the door.

The Brute was lying on the bed.

'Did I tell you you could leave the bathroom?' he asked.

'Is Lauryn gone?' Colm asked, ignoring the question.

'No, she's hiding under the bed.'

Colm sat down. He wished she hadn't left. He still hadn't managed to get her to explain the curse. It was starting to gnaw away at him and he needed to talk about it.

'I have a problem,' The Brute said.

Colm sighed with relief. The Brute may be, well, brutish, but he wasn't going to let his cousin down when he was in trouble. He was there when Colm had run his fingers along the spine of *The Book of Dread*. He was there when Lauryn said it was cursed. He knew what Colm was worried about. Good old Brute. On his side at last. He'd help him in his hour of need.

Wait, he'd said 'I have a problem'. He meant 'We have a problem', didn't he?

'What's wrong?' Colm asked.

'Lauryn likes books.'

Oh. He did mean he had a problem after all. Looked like Colm was going to have to deal with things by himself.

'So what if she likes books?' he asked, unable to keep the annoyance out of his voice.

'I've never read a book in my life,' said The Brute. He almost sounded proud when he said it.

'When you say never ...'

'Not once.'

'Except for the novels you read in school. For English, I mean,' Colm said.

'Jeez, you're supposed to be smart. When I said never, I meant it. I never read one, not even those boring ones in school. I'd either copy the homework or sometimes I'd get a DVD of the book,' said The Brute. He tapped his forehead. 'It's called thinking. I'm not thick, you know.'

'I never said you were,' said Colm.

'But you think it.'

This wasn't entirely untrue, which is to say it was mainly true. The Brute never struck Colm as someone who'd win Mastermind when he grew up.

'I don't see what this has got to do with me,' Colm said.

The Brute sighed. 'It's not difficult, Uggo. Lauryn is gorgeous. I fancy her. If she thinks we like the same things then she'll like me. Then she becomes girlfriend number thirty-three for Michael "Superdude" McGrath.'

'Is that how you get a girlfriend – by pretending to be different from who you really are?'

'Works every time. Anyway, you know books. Teach me,' said The Brute.

'But that's not fair. You'll be tricking her into liking you.'

The Brute pointed to himself. 'You see this? You see this face? This is the face of someone who doesn't care.' He looked at his watch. 'We have twenty minutes. Tell me everything you know about books. Stuff that makes me look like I read all the time. Unless you have a problem with that?'

He cracked his knuckles.

Colm gulped. Twice.

'No problem at all,' he squeaked.

·•◆•·

The next twenty minutes flew by. Much to his surprise, Colm was having fun. He told his cousin everything he knew about books, which was a lot, and The Brute memorised everything he could, which wasn't very much. It was the first time they'd had a proper conversation. It almost felt like they were friends.

Until The Brute said, 'Thanks for the info, Jessica.'

Calling him a girl's name. That was a new one.

'We'd better go down to the restaurant,' Colm said. 'Mam'll go mad if we're late.'

'I'm not going,' said The Brute. 'I've got things to do.'

Colm assumed that the things included hanging out with Lauryn.

'What'll I say to Mam?' he asked.

'I don't care,' said The Brute. 'Make up an excuse, but make it a good one.'

'OK,' Colm said.

He opened the bedroom door but hesitated before he left.

'Can I ask you something?'

'Go on,' said The Brute with a sigh.

'Do you remember what Lauryn said earlier about the book being cursed?'

The Brute nodded.

'Do you believe what she said?' Colm asked.

'I don't believe in curses. Or fairies or leprechauns or goblins or witches. Don't tell me you're scared?'

'Of course I'm not,' Colm lied.

'That's typical of you,' said The Brute. 'Just sitting there all worried. If it was me I'd be out there getting answers. When you have a problem you can do one of two things – you can either feel sorry for yourself or you can take action. That's what my dad always says.'

'That doesn't sound like something Seanie'd say.'

'Seanie's not my dad,' he shouted.

Colm ducked as a pillow hit the wall.

'See you later,' he said shutting the door behind him.

·◆·

The Book of Dread (4)

April 13th, 1896

The Lazarus Key exists! In fact, at one stage there were three of them. I can hardly believe it. I have spent days in the great libraries of Dublin and found numerous references to it. My uncle is furious with me. He says that I have failed him by not having the hotel ready as promised, but I do not care. If I find the Key I shall be a rich man. It is worth thousands of pounds.

According to my research the first record of the Key was in a remote area of Asia in the third century. It was worshipped by an obscure religious cult known as the Ruksza. They used the Key in battles against their barbaric neighbours and believed the Key had great powers. Whoever holds the Key will not die. If they are fatally wounded they will return to life.

Attila the Hun was said to have stolen one of the Keys and his army was so terrified of him coming back after his death that he was buried in a triple coffin of gold, silver and iron beneath a riverbed. Of course I do not believe this magical nonsense, but the stories will only add to the value of the Key when I find it and sell it to a collector or a museum.

The Key is even mentioned in the stories of Genghis Khan. The Ruksza were the only tribe in their region that the great warlord failed to conquer. The legends said that when his armies knew of the presence of the Key they refused to wage war upon them.

In the Kildare Street library I met a Mr Stoker who, upon seeing the books I was reading, became most animated. He was on holiday from London and said he had heard of the Key during the course of his own research for a novel he has written which will be published next year. He said that in Romania the terrible ruler, Vlad the Impaler, came back to life after his death with the aid of a Key. I must return to the Red House and find the Key. Immediately.

Seven

'Can you zoom in?' Cedric asked.

'You tell me. It's your laptop,' said the security woman, but then she added, 'No. If we zoom in we lose quality.'

They were in a small office at Shannon airport. Too small for Cedric, Kate and the security woman to fit in all at once, so Kate had left, supposedly to talk to someone who might be able to help them, but Cedric suspected it was also to have a crafty smoke.

The busy sound of cars, taxis and buses, and the noisy chatter of passengers drifted in through the open window. But it was still roasting in the office and Cedric felt far too hot and very uncomfortable.

'Could you not have found somewhere bigger than this place?' he asked.

'I'll tell you what, Cedric – why don't we go to the Garda

office? I hear it has nice comfortable chairs and it's very spacious and airy. While we're there we can tell them how I illegally downloaded CCTV footage from the airport's security cameras while my pig-headed boss was on a toilet break, then rang you on your mobile to tell you about it and while I waited for you to drive down from Dublin I put the images on a CD which I'm going to give you in exchange for money. I'm sure they'd love to know all that. Then when we're both in prison you can tell me if your cell is bigger than this office,' the security woman said.

'A simple yes or no would have done,' said Cedric. 'Are you always this crabby?'

'Only when I meet you. You bring out the worst in me.'

'I have that effect on a lot of people. Natural charm, I suppose.'

The footage on the computer's monitor was in freeze-frame. The picture was a little grainy, but as far as Cedric could make out it was the man he was looking for all right. Looked like wasn't good enough though. He needed to be certain.

'When was this taken?'

'Tuesday.'

Two days ago. The timing was right.

'Can you run it for me again?' he asked.

'What's the magic word?'

'Abracadabra.'

The security woman wasn't amused.

'Please,' sighed Cedric.

She moved her fingers over the computer's pad then clicked on the rewind button on the screen. The people moved backwards in a jerky motion. They looked like puppets being controlled by someone up above. The woman pressed play and all the people on the monitor moved forward.

Cedric leaned in close to the screen, but the closer he got the more out of focus the image seemed. He rubbed his eyes.

'Just one more time.'

The security woman rewound the footage again and pressed the play button. Cedric watched the tall, thin man look up at the camera for the briefest of moments, then he seemed to realise what he'd done and covered his face with his hand. Definitely suspicious.

'He seems to know the two in front of him,' Cedric said.

'If you say so.'

He watched as the tall, thin man vanished from the screen. Two-day-old CCTV footage. That's all they had to go on. If it was the wrong man and they ended up following him, they could waste valuable hours and all the while the little rat-faced man would be waiting for him. Waiting for him to make a mistake.

'Ced, got a moment?' Kate said, sticking her head around the door.

'I'll be back in a minute,' he said to the security woman.

'I can't wait,' she replied in a voice dripping with sarcasm.

Cedric stepped outside and breathed in the exhaust fumes of the passing traffic. At least the air was cooler out here.

'Tell me you've got good news, Kate,' he said.

'Depends on what you mean by good news.'

'The only good news I could get at the moment is that we've found our man.'

'We haven't found him.'

'Thanks Kate, you dragged me out here to tell me we *haven't* found him. Well, isn't that brilliant. What are you going to tell me next? You've figured out that the big orange disc in the sky disappears at night?'

'If you're trying to be funny, you're not.'

'Really? Tell me something I don't know.'

'How about this one? I know how we *can* find him.'

Cedric was so happy he wanted to kiss her. He didn't of course, partly because it would be an uncomfortable, awkward moment for both of them. Mainly though, because he knew that if he kissed her she'd hit him. And not just a gentle slap on the face. It'd be a big, juicy nose-breaker.

·◆·

Unlike the small security office, the car-hire building was bright and airy and filled with glum people who were fed up waiting to get their cars. They were even more fed up when Cedric and Kate jumped the queue and went to the top of the line.

'Hey, I was here first,' said a bald-headed businessman as they shoved past him.

Kate glared at him. 'Excuse me?'

'I hadn't finished my sentence,' gulped the businessman. 'I was here first, but I'd be delighted to let you two go ahead of me.'

'That's very kind of you,' said Kate. She smiled and the businessman shuddered. He had never seen a more terrifying sight in his life.

'This is Mark,' said Kate introducing the man behind the counter.

'Thanks. I'd never have been able to read his name tag,' Cedric said.

Mark was skinny and wore far too much hair gel. It was like he'd dipped his head in a tub of grease before he left for work.

'Mark, tell my colleague Cedric the Sarcastic what you just told me.'

'Not here,' said Mark. He put a sign on his desk that read 'Back in five minutes' amid groans from the rest of the queue and led Kate and Cedric back outside.

'What have you got for me?' Cedric asked.

Mark looked nervously around him in case someone was watching them.

'It's not a spy drama, Mark. Nobody's interested in us.'

'Oh,' he said, disappointed. His job was very boring and he was enjoying feeling like he was part of something exciting. He handed them a printed page. 'This is a photocopy of the driver's licence of a man who hired a car from us two days ago,' he said.

Cedric studied the picture.

'It's him, isn't it, the guy from the photo?' Kate said.

'Looks like him all right,' Cedric agreed. 'Have you got the make, model and registration plate of the car he hired?'

'Better than that,' Mark said smugly.

Cedric waited for him to finish, but he saw that Mark wanted his moment in the sun. 'Better than that? Wow, that's amazing, Mark. What have you got?' he asked without enthusiasm.

'He hired a luxury car. All our luxury cars are fitted with GPS,' he said. 'That stands for global positioning system. It means we know where the car is at all times.'

He saw the look on Cedric's face.

'There wasn't any need for me to explain that, was there?'

'No, but please carry on,' Cedric said through gritted teeth.

'The car was driven south the day it was hired. It didn't travel far after that. Never more than outside a two-mile radius of this location.' He handed Cedric another page. 'It's been parked there for the last seven hours.'

This time Cedric was impressed. 'Is there a chance that this information could be wrong?'

'Absolutely not. We only use the best of equipment and it's constantly checked by one of our technicians,' Mark said.

'That's excellent work. Thank you very much for your help,' said Cedric in his most pleasant voice.

'Ahm.'

'Yes, Mark?'

'The lady said that you'd, you know, pay me if I told you what I knew,' he said.

'But we have all the information. Why would I bother paying you now?' Cedric asked.

Mark's face fell. He looked like he was about to cry.

'Nah, I'm only messing with you. How much did you promise him, Kate?'

'Fifty euro.'

Cedric took out his wallet. 'Here's a hundred,' he said handing over the money. He gave him his business card. 'My mobile number's on the card. That car even moves an inch, you give me a call. And if your information is accurate there'll be another two hundred in it for you.'

'Yes, Mr Murphy. Thank you,' Mark beamed.

'Let's go,' Cedric said to Kate.

Mark began to move off in the opposite direction.

'Aren't you going to go back into your office?' Kate asked him.

'Nah, I'm off on my break. That lot of whingers can wait,' Mark replied.

'One other question. Was the man alone?' Cedric asked.

'No, there were two others with him. Not the sort that you'd forget either,' said Mark with a wink.

·◆·

The Book of Dread (5)

April 14th, 1896

Before I left for the Red House I met with Mr
Stoker again. We talked in a teahouse on George's
Street. He showed me some notes he had made
on the Lazarus Key. When he was paying for
our teas I stole them and ran from the place. I
could hear him shouting after me, but I did not
care. A short time later I took the train south.

The journey passed quickly as I read his
notes. One of the Keys was in America in
the earlier part of the century. It was in the
possession of a vicious gang of thugs in Boston.
They were known as the Sign of Lazarus
and every ne'er-do-well member of the gang
had their symbol – a diamond inside a skull
– tattooed on their finger or the inner part of
their arm. They ruled the city with a fist of
iron and were as cruel as one's imagination
allows. But then the Key was stolen from
them! If my drunken friend from the public
house was telling the truth, then I believe I
know who the thief was.

Upon my return to the Red House I found
my uncle there. He is now overseeing the

project, but he would not allow me into the house. He tried to attack me with his walking stick, but I ran away. Later, after nightfall, I crept into the house. It was dark and cold and though I do not like to admit it, I was afraid. Not of my uncle, but of the house itself. There is an eerie feeling about the Red House once darkness falls. I crept into the cellar and by candlelight I found a treasure chest of papers belonging to the family who once owned this house – the DeLancey-O'Brien's. The papers have confirmed what I suspected. I must take some time to order my thoughts. When I have things clear in my head I will begin my search. Soon I will be rich and I shall laugh in my uncle's face.

Eight

There were fifteen tables in the restaurant and fourteen of them were empty, but every one of them was still laid out as if guests were going to arrive at any moment. Soft music played in the background; nothing Colm recognised, but it was the sort of thing his mother must have liked because she hummed along. His father held a wine glass up to the light as if searching for some sign of dirt or dust.

'Put it down, Joe,' said Colm's mother. Her lips were thin when she spoke. Never a good sign.

She didn't want her husband embarrassing her in a nice place like this. Even though she spoke quietly her voice seemed to echo around the room.

'The tablecloths are lovely. High quality linen. We should get some,' she said. Her husband and son looked at her blankly. Sometimes it was hard for her being the only woman in the house. Nobody ever really talked about the things she was interested in.

'Where's Michael? I thought he'd be down by now,' Colm's father said.

'I warned him not to be late,' said his mother, looking at her watch.

'He's not coming down for dinner,' Colm said.

'And why not?'

Make it a good lie, Colm thought.

'He's sick. He's in the bathroom,' he said. On a scale of one to ten that lie was a one. It was rubbish, but it was out there now. It would have to do.

'Has he been vomiting?' his mother asked.

'No, the other thing.'

'The other thing? Oh, you mean … Oh.'

Not something any of them wanted to think about.

'Maybe I should go and see if he's all right,' she said, getting up from her chair.

Colm's dad placed a hand on her arm. 'Better to leave it, love. You don't want to embarrass the boy,' he said.

'I won't embarrass him. I'll be very discreet,' she said.

'I'll check on him in a minute. It'd be better if I did it,' Colm said quickly.

'I don't know,' said his mother, still unsure.

'Colm's right,' said his dad. 'I know teenage boys. I was

one once. They're fierce easy to embarrass. Colm can go up in a few minutes.'

'Mmm, OK. I suppose you're right. It was probably those chips he ate. I told you that roadside café was filthy.'

The waiter – who was the porter dressed in a different uniform – arrived and took their order. His new clothes didn't appear to make him any happier. He managed to take the whole order without speaking once. He just nodded curtly and wrote things down in his little black note-book.

'I gave him twenty euro already so that covers the tip for the meal as well,' said Colm's father when the porter-waiter had gone back into the kitchen.

The meal was more like a work of art than a dinner. It looked great but there wasn't much of it. Colm didn't care. Even if it had been his favourite – double cheeseburger, chips and curried beans – he wouldn't have had much of an appetite. He had other things on his mind.

His mother seemed to like it though. She was smiling and even holding his father's hand from time to time when she thought Colm wasn't looking.

Colm wolfed down the meal because he knew if he didn't his mother would start asking awkward questions. It didn't take too long to finish. A sparrow with a small appetite could have scoffed it and not ended up with a swollen belly.

He was about to ask if he could leave the table when the porter-waiter brought the dessert menu.

·◆·

The Brute looked at his watch for the tenth time in the last nine minutes. He was nervous. He checked his armpits. Still not a whiff. Good. Not a night for him to stink. He paced up and down the bedroom measuring the distance from the window to the door for no particular reason. Fourteen steps.

He bit his nails. Checked himself out in the mirror. Apart from a couple of spots on his chin and one unsqueezable monster right at the corner of his nose, he was looking good.

Still no sign of Lauryn. He began to worry that she might not show up. It wasn't a date, so he couldn't really be stood up, but he didn't want to be rejected. He couldn't take that.

Not again.

In the last twelve months he'd asked thirteen girls out and they'd all said no. Even Una Ryan. And she'd gone out with Johnny the Goat with the stupid laugh. Typical. Of course he'd told Colm that he'd had thirty-two girlfriends and he'd believed him. The dope.

At least he wasn't here to see him fail miserably. He probably wouldn't say anything even if he was. He'd just look at him stupidly and maybe even feel sorry for him. There was nothing worse than that.

He couldn't stand waiting any longer. He had to get out. Do something. The room was far too stuffy and warm. Maybe if he let in some fresh air. He looped his fingers around the sash hooks on the window and heaved it up. Cool, clean air rushed into the room. That was better. He felt refreshed. He fastened the window so that it stayed open and was about to go and brush his teeth for the third time when he spotted the small figure far down below at the edge of the woods. Was that Lauryn? It looked like her.

'Lauryn. Up here,' he called.

She didn't look up. She probably couldn't hear him. The figure, if it was Lauryn, took a few steps to her left and disappeared into the woods. The Brute hesitated for a split second before he made his decision. He'd go after her.

He ran out of the room and down the stairs, three at a time. He sprinted across the foyer and out into the courtyard, where he stopped for a moment. OK, he thought, our room is at the back of the hotel, so that's where she went into the woods.

He passed through a small garden, all shrubs and flowers, leaped over a low hedge and passed a navy BMW that was parked around the back.

He stopped and looked up to check where his room was. Second storey, fourth room from the left, which meant

Lauryn was just about where he was standing now when he last saw her. The woods were quiet and there was no sign of her, but he saw her footprints on the soft mud of the path. He followed on, not sure if it was a good idea. It made him look like a weirdo, following her like this, so he called out: 'Lauryn. Hey. It's me, Michael. Wait up.'

His voice reverberated through the trees, but there was no reply. Just silence. Decision time again. Should he keep going or turn back? He kept going. He wasn't a quitter. He moved further into the woods and even though he could see some of the fading daylight through the tops of the trees, it had already begun to get dark where he was. The mud was ruining his new trainers too. He thought he saw a movement off to his left. A shadow in the trees.

That must be her.

'Lauryn,' he called out again. There was no reply other than his own voice echoing back at him.

He broke into a jog. He was a good runner and he was certain he'd catch up with her easily, but after a few minutes he still hadn't spotted her. How had she slipped away from him so quickly?

·•◆•·

He'd gone much deeper into the woods now and when he looked back he couldn't see the top of the hotel any more.

That wasn't good. He hoped he wouldn't get lost. That would be embarrassing. He'd rather spend the night out here in the cold and dark than shout for help.

He thought he felt something brush against his foot, but when he looked down there was nothing there. He hoped it wasn't a rat. He was terrified of them. He'd told Mrs McMahon that if he found one in the hotel that he'd take care of it, but the thought of seeing a rat almost made him sick.

He looked around. He was in amongst the scrub grass and brambles now, and he realised with a growing horror that he'd drifted off the path. That wasn't clever. He tried to think. Could he remember when he'd left the path? Nope. This wasn't good.

He'd seen a horror film once with his dad. The people had accidentally left a path when they were in some creepy part of the English countryside and they'd been attacked by werewolves. His mam had come in halfway through the film and given out to his dad for letting him watch it. She'd said he was far too young. Typical. She was always trying to ruin his fun. It was a good film, but the thought of it didn't cheer him up. OK, there was no such thing as werewolves, but even thinking of them made him shiver. He kept walking and it kept getting darker.

Brilliant.

The woods were much larger than he'd imagined. From

the hotel bedroom window they'd looked small enough, but now that he was down here among the trees and briers he began to wonder if he'd just made a huge mistake. Wouldn't be the first time.

Which way had he come from? It was difficult to make anything out, but he must be close to the river – he was certain he could hear the sound of running water. Well, if the river was that way, then the hotel was in the opposite direction. Had to be.

He set off back in the direction he thought he'd come from, but there was still no sign of the path and it really was getting dark. And cold. He hoped Lauryn wasn't stuck out here too. She'd probably be scared if she was. What was she doing in here anyway? He hadn't thought of that before. Was she just going for a walk? Who went for walks on their own? Middle-aged women and other boring people. Not gorgeous teenagers. Unless she was looking for something. But what could she be looking for?

'Lauryn. Can you hear me?' he shouted. No reply.

He crossed his fingers. 'Let her be OK,' he thought. Then he reminded himself that this was her grandmother's hotel and she probably knew the woods like the back of her hand.

The brambles grew thicker as The Brute carried on in the wrong direction. After a while he knew that there was no need to wonder any longer if he might be lost. He was.

Hopelessly so. In the distance there was a crack of thunder and then he heard the first trickle of rain on the leaves. A big fat drop landed right on his head with an annoying plop. Just when you think things can't get any worse they always do, he said to himself.

He felt tired and miserable and stupid. He could imagine Colm lying cosy and warm in the hotel room with the central heating on full blast. Probably eating a bar of chocolate too.

•◆•

Colm was cosy and warm and he was eating chocolate, but it was a chocolate dessert. He finished it and asked to be excused.

'Are you going to check on Michael?' his mother asked.

'Yeah,' he lied.

'Thanks Colm,' she said.

That made him feel guilty, but not for long. Before he had the chance to leave the table Mrs McMahon called over to see how they were getting on.

'It's a beautiful meal. Delicious,' said Colm's mother. 'And thank you again for getting the chef in at such short notice. He can't have been too happy to have been called in on his day off.'

'Ah, sure that fella's never happy. If he won a million euro on the Lotto he'd be moaning that the lad that won it the week before got two million. He can grumble if he wants, but he'll grumble himself out of a job if he's not careful. So, do you like the rooms?'

'They're fabulous. Very comfortable, aren't they, Joe?'

Colm's father grunted a reply.

'Well, if you want anything, just give me a call. Sure, I've nothing else to be doing.'

'Thank you, we will. I hope we didn't get your daughter in trouble by just turning up like this.'

'Yerra, we had a big blowout and she went off in a huff, but she's been like that ever since she was a child. A crier and a sulker. It was all a misunderstanding.' She winked at Colm as if to say 'remember our little secret', then shuffled off to the kitchen.

'Will we get another bottle of wine, Joe?' Colm's mother asked.

He could see his father was about to complain about the cost of the wine – posh wine is always expensive, especially in restaurants – but for once his dad held his tongue.

'Go on. Since we're out for the night we may as well enjoy ourselves. You'll come down and tell us if Michael isn't feeling better soon, right?'

'Will do. See you later,' Colm said.

•◆•

He didn't go back to the hotel room. Instead he wandered through the lobby trying to look like he didn't have a care in the world. Act casual, he told himself. Look as if you're just strolling about. He stuffed his hands in his jeans pockets and tried a jaunty whistle. But there was nobody around, so his little ruse was unnecessary. With a quick look behind him, just to be sure, he snuck into the library. There was nobody in there either and it would have felt creepy if it wasn't so hot; the central heating was on full blast.

He stood before the book. He wasn't sure why he was doing this, but The Brute was right – he couldn't just sit around doing nothing. If the book was cursed then he'd have to find out more about it. And if it wasn't then what had he got to lose? He'd already touched the book once, so there was no harm having a proper look at it. You couldn't be cursed twice, right?

He took a deep breath, reached out and grabbed it from the shelf. It was lighter than it looked. The cover was scratched and stained, as if someone had spilled a cup of tea or coffee on it many years before.

He sat down in one of the leather armchairs – no point in being uncomfortable – and opened it. The first few pages were like a scrapbook. Yellowed newspaper cuttings about the opening of the hotel. Nothing too interesting there. He glanced over them then turned a few more pages until he found what he was looking for. The writing was thin and spidery, but just about clear enough to read. It was a diary of some sort. It told the story of a man who over a hundred years ago had been here to do some work on the hotel. He read through the diary entries until he reached the final few.

•◆•

The Book of Dread (6)

April 15th, 1896

I have pieced the puzzle together! In 1817 the Red House was owned by a rich family known as the DeLancey-O'Brien's. They had a son, Hugh, and everyone agreed there was something strange about the boy. He was a cruel child given to fits of vile temper. He was unusual in appearance too – his eyes blazed red around the rim of his pupils giving him a fearsome look. An accident at the age of eleven left him with a scar running from the corner of his eye to his mouth. If he was a bad child, he was a brutish adult. He spent his days horse riding – his long black hair flowing behind him, his red eyes blazing – and his nights drinking and fighting. Whenever people in the village heard his horse's hooves on the road they hid in their houses. At night he would prowl the streets of the village with his only friend, a giant, black dog who was as mean-tempered as his master, looking for trouble.

He grew bored of the countryside and his black heart longed for excitement and adventure, for even though he was merciless and spiteful, he was also brave and wild. He begged his father for some money so that he could travel the world and make his own fortune. His father agreed, yet he didn't know that when he waved him farewell one cold winter's morning that he would never see his son again, for it would be ten years before Hugh returned and his father was dead by then.

There was a knock at my door. My heart leapt, but it was only the owner of the inn telling me my supper was ready. I am nervous these days, yet I don't know why. I should not be fearful when my fortune will soon be in my hands, yet every sound, every whisper frightens me. I shall continue my writing after I have eaten.

One hour later:

I have just had a most awful meal of boiled cabbage and cow's tongue. When I am rich I shall eat like a king. Where was I? Ah, yes.

Nobody knows for certain what Hugh did when he left Ireland. Once or twice a year his family would get a letter from some foreign land in which Hugh would tell them of the adventures he was having. Nothing was heard from him for almost eighteen months until his family received a letter from Africa. Hugh was excited. He said that he had little money left, but he had a feeling that he was about to make a fortune if his luck held. He wrote of a treasure he had heard about from a penniless ex-soldier he'd met on a sea voyage. I have found his letter among the items stored in the treasure chest in the Red House:

He is a low-born fellow of indeterminate age and of an appearance that is both displeasing to the eye and to the nostrils. The creature is riddled with cankers and sores. It sickened me to spend any time in his presence and at first I wanted nothing more than to be rid of his company. The wretch begged me for money. He held out his hands like one of those wastrel supplicants that have bedevilled my travels. Yet, though I was tempted to thrash him to within an inch of his miserable life, I noticed he bore a strange mark in Indian ink upon his index finger. I have seen this mark once before and I know what it represents – it is

the Sign of Lazarus. I questioned him and
for a few shillings the fool revealed all to
me. It disgusted me to find how easily he
gave up his clan's secrets. Nevertheless, it
was a most interesting tale and it took all
my fortitude to stop myself crying out in
delight and excitement. After he finished
he swore we were now blood brothers. I
did not enlighten him as to how unlike
brothers we are, how his kind are more
akin to rats than to the proud DeLancey-
O'Briens. I let him believe that we were
bound by blood because the creature will
be of some use to me, as he knows the New
World and I do not. We are to set sail for
Boston on the morrow. The task that lies
ahead of us is filled with peril but, if I
succeed, when I return I shall have riches
beyond compare (the poor fellow believes
that we shall share these riches) and the
name of DeLancey-O'Brien shall once
again ring around the world.

April 19th, 1896

I have been lax in the upkeep of my diary
since I attached the copy of Hugh's letter. Too
much has happened. My mind has been in constant turmoil. Darkness is all around me and
I would rather be anywhere else in the world

than where I am now. For the sake of innocents everywhere I must record what happened to Hugh DeLancey-O'Brien.

After the last letter his family never received another communication. They worried about Hugh and contacted everyone they knew in important positions in America, but he was never found. In the end they presumed he was dead, killed in his pursuit of the unknown treasure.

Then one day, a year after Hugh's father had died, his mother was sitting in the library when she saw a stranger in rags walking towards the house. He appeared to her to be an elderly beggar and she went outside with a blackthorn stick in her hand to confront the vagrant. She was shocked when the old black dog of Hugh's slowly padded up to the stranger and began to lick his hand. He usually attacked anyone who called to the house, even after his teeth had rotted away and he could barely walk.

'Who are you?' she called out to the man.

His hair was long and grey, he was missing an eye and he walked in a shambling manner.

'Mother, don't you recognise your own child?' asked Hugh.

She could hardly believe it. It was her son. He was only twenty-nine and he looked like a sixty-year-old. She took him in and nursed him back to health and though his appearance improved he was a man who was forever changed.

When he had regained his strength he began to take walks in the village, but where once he'd have picked a fight with anyone he met, now he shunned all contact. He seemed to fear every shadow, every sudden noise. He was a broken man.

In the safety of his home he sat silently for hours on end and when he did talk it was always something about the village or the land; he refused to say anything about his travels. He grew angry at the mere mention of his time abroad. Nobody knew what had happened to him in America, although sometimes the servants would be woken at night by his screams. When they'd go to his room to calm him down he'd stare at them with wild eyes and say 'The Lazarus Key. Why did I ever involve myself with the Lazarus Key?' And night after night he'd sit by the fire trying to rub off a sign that had been tattooed onto his finger – a diamond with a horrible skull at its centre.

Years passed and he began to grow calmer, but he was always terrified of strangers. If he heard of a visitor in the village, he'd lock himself away in his room until he was assured that all was safe. 'They'll find me. Maybe not now, but some day they'll come back for it,' he'd say in a whisper.

He lived a long and unhappy life and when he died a maid was given the job of sorting through his things. She found a locked trunk in his room. Being a curious girl, she broke the lock and found that there was nothing in there other than a leather pouch. Inside the pouch was a small object. That evening she became unnaturally giddy, but shortly afterwards complained of feeling ill. She was found dead in her bed the next morning. The object was placed in Hugh DeLancey-O'Brien's hand prior to burial. Several mourners said that they saw his hands move and a light come to his eyes. There were reports that the undertaker, the only other person known to have touched the blasted thing, came to a horrible end shortly afterwards, but I have been unable to verify that.

Date Unknown

My hands tremble as I write these words by candlelight. I do not know what day it is. Even the month and year elude me at this moment. I hear the men and women laughing in the next room and I envy them. If what I have

discovered about this place is true then I shall
be dead before first light. How I wish that I had
never come here. My name is of no concern.
My life is of no consequence. I only write to
warn others. Beware of the Key of Lazarus.

My foolish thoughts led me to believe that if
I could locate the Key I could sell it and make
my fortune. I was convinced that it would be
worth a vast sum of money. As for the tales
I had heard about the Key, I did not believe
them. I am a man of reason and I ~~do not~~ did
not believe in magick. I thought the stories
were arrant nonsense, ghost stories of the type
you will find in any town or village in Ireland.
I was wrong. Most dreadfully wrong. Fate was
about to play its cruellest trick upon me.

Night after night I snuck back to the Red
House after my uncle and his workers had left
and I searched for the Key. I became a man
possessed. My hair, once neatly combed, grew
long and unruly, my beard unkempt. I did not
sleep. After weeks of searching, I uncovered
the Key of Lazarus. I will not relay to you
where it rested. I do not want some other poor
misfortunate to follow me down this dreadful
path. When I held the Key in my hand I felt
my heart leap with joy. I was consumed with
a happiness I never knew could exist in this
world. The happiness stayed only for an hour.

The sickness followed. Now I know the truth. The Key is most powerful. If you take it in your hand it draws the very life from your body. You begin to fade away. And then the one who has power over the Key follows its signal. It will take the Key and steal all of your life from the wretched object. That is why the thing does not die. It feeds on the lives of others. I know this now. I know that the Key is in the wrong hands. It must be destroyed but I do not know how to destroy it. Instead all I can do is wait.

As I look out the window I see that dawn is less than an hour away. It will be here shortly. To take the Key and take my life. It cannot stand the light or walk in the day like a human, for while it was once human it is not any more. I do not know what else to write. Hark, I hear it. Its feet drag across the hall floor in a manner that chills me to the very depths of my soul. It is coming for me. I see the handle of the door begin to turn. It is nearly here. I cannot bear to look up from my page. It is in the room. I can smell its foul stench. My time on this earth is at an end. These are my final words. Do not search for it. Do not desire it. Run. Run for your life and never stop when you hear of the Key of L

a

z

Nine

The writing ended there, the words unfinished. Colm closed the book. That was a cheery read, he thought. While he'd been reading *The Book of Dread* it was as if he'd been transported to another time, long since past, and now it felt peculiar to be sitting here in the comfortable armchair as the rain pelted against the window.

He wondered what had happened to the man who wrote the book. It didn't look good. Had the creature got him? And if so, what was the creature? And what was the Key? Could it really bring someone back from the dead? He shuddered at the thought.

He flicked through the book again to see if there was anything that he'd missed. Anything that might tell him what had happened here in the Red House Hotel. Maybe even in this very room.

There was no other clue as to what had happened to the man. Nothing about the creature. Nothing about the Lazarus Key.

There was one bit of good news though. Unless he was hugely mistaken *The Book of Dread* wasn't cursed. Everything the man had written in the book said that those who held the Lazarus Key in their hand died before the first light of the following morning. Not the book, the Key.

No, *The Book of Dread* wasn't something to worry about. Lauryn must have got it wrong. Or else she was playing a trick on him. The book was fine. As long as he stayed clear of the Lazarus Key everything would be all right. And he had no intention of looking for it.

·◆·

The Brute's path was blocked with briers. He stomped down on them and carried on, but after a while they grew so high and tough that it was difficult to push through. It was obvious to him that no one had been here in years. It was too overgrown. The brambles were thick and strong and grew around each other and in a criss-cross pattern. He covered his hand with the sleeve of his jacket and pushed at the thorns, but they barely moved. He tried it a few times, but each time he was as successful as the last, which is to say completely unsuccessful. He grew more and more frustrated.

The anger built up inside of him until it was a bubbling rage. Finally he let out a roar and swung his right leg high in the air and brought the heel of his trainer smashing down on top of the brambles. Some of them broke and the others were smooshed down enough for him to step over.

'Superdude 1, Nature 0,' he said with a smile.

He had no idea where he was now, but the rain was bucketing down and he was getting soaked. He pulled his jacket tighter round him, but it wasn't offering much protection. He called out Lauryn's name again, but just as before there was no answer. No sound except the rain splashing on the ground.

He needed somewhere to shelter from the downpour. He stood against the bark of an ash tree, but the water just dripped from the leaves and rolled down the back of his neck. He'd have to find somewhere better. Maybe if he dashed across to that tree over there. The big one. He didn't know the names of any trees. He hadn't paid attention in primary school when they were learning all that nature stuff. He'd been too busy firing spitwads at the back of Alan Murphy's head. What did it matter now? Knowing the name of the tree wouldn't make it a better shelter. How far was it? Ten yards? Fifteen? He'd sprint it.

Halfway there his foot caught in something and sent him sprawling. He slid through the wet the leaves and only came to a stop when his arm got caught on a thorny branch. He heard his jacket rip. He got to his feet and inspected the damage. The right arm of the jacket was torn and the lining was poking out. The knees of his jeans were drenched and covered in some sort of slime. His hands were filthy and he was certain he'd chipped a tooth. Why did everything bad have to happen to him?

What had tripped him? He wanted to kick it. It wouldn't do any good, but it'd make him feel a lot better. Before he'd even had the chance to look he heard someone call his name.

'Michael.' The voice was soft, yet rasping.

'Hello?' The Brute called out. He couldn't make out which direction the voice was coming from.

'Hello. Lauryn, is that you? Are you hurt or something?'

'Michael.'

It didn't sound like her. Not at all. But who else could it be? There wouldn't be anybody else in the woods who'd know his name. Unless it was Colm. The little twerp wouldn't have followed him, would he? Surely not. He was scared of his own shadow, that fella. But what if he had? His cousin was annoying, but he didn't like the thought of him being stuck out here. Even he didn't deserve that.

'Colm,' he said. 'Is that you?'

'Help me,' said the voice.

The words seemed to be coming from nearby. As if …
no, that was a stupid thought. But even so, The Brute had
to admit that it sounded as if they were coming from under
the ground.

He dropped to his knees. The rain teemed down but he
didn't notice it anymore. If one of his family, even Colm,
was in trouble he wasn't going to leave them there. That
wasn't how it worked.

The forest floor was a mess of overgrown brambles and
weeds.

'Where are you?' The Brute asked.

'You'll find me,' said the voice.

No, it didn't sound like Colm at all. Unless he was weak
and injured. Maybe that's why he sounded different.

He tore away at the weeds and briers, pulling them out
of the ground with his bare hands. Soon his fingers were
cut to shreds but The Brute didn't even notice the blood
dripping from them. He worked in a frenzy, clawing at the
weeds, dragging the briers out and throwing them over his
shoulder. Finally he felt something.

He bent down to have a closer look. It was a ring of some
sort. A thick metal ring bigger than his hand. What was
that doing here in the middle of a wood? He lifted it up,
but it didn't come very far. It was attached to something. If
he didn't know better he'd think it was a trapdoor. He did

know better and it was still a trapdoor. He pulled at it. It was stuck.

The rain began to gather in pools around his feet. He gave the metal handle another tug. Nothing doing. How had Colm managed to get himself imprisoned under there? He didn't have time to think about that.

He swept his hand around it, breaking through the weeds and moss until he found what he was looking for – a groove in the soil. The outline of the door. He tore the last of the moss away – how long had it been growing for – centuries? – until he could see it clearly. It was about two feet square. Not much room for someone of his size to squeeze through. Why was there a trapdoor in the middle of the woods?

'Hold on. I'll be there in a minute,' he shouted.

He grabbed the ring with both hands. He heard his father's words in his head – let the legs do the work, save your back. His father was a builder and well used to lifting things. He was a real man, not like Bald Seanie. All he ever lifted was a pen to correct homework.

The Brute pulled with all his might. He could feel his face grow red with the effort and his legs began to buckle, but the thing didn't move. Not even an inch.

He relaxed, took a deep breath, and tried again. This time he made progress. He heard the roots of whatever plants had grown around it ripping and screeching as they were torn away. Come on, he told himself, you can do it. Captain of the hurling team. Captain of the rugby team. Undefeated in five school fights and fifteen after-school fights. No one could beat him. No one. His teeth ground together. He could feel his shoulders begin to burn as if they were going to be ripped from their sockets. He let his mind wander to a different place. Block out the pain.

The trapdoor began to open, centimetre by agonising centimetre, but he was already exhausted. He felt the strength drain from him. His arms began to shake with the effort. The handle slipping through his fingers.

'Come on, Michael,' he shouted, but it was no good. He was losing the battle.

Then from somewhere deep down inside of him he felt the strength return. It was an odd feeling. Not like when he was wrecked in a rugby match and got a second wind. This was different. As if somebody was helping him even though there was nobody there.

He felt a surge of power sweep through him.

And suddenly he was sitting on his rear end and the trapdoor was open. He didn't even remember the last thirty seconds. He just sat there letting the rain wash over him. He didn't feel like himself. He slapped himself on the face and shook off the feeling.

He got to his feet and peered down into the gaping maw below and saw absolutely nothing. It was too dark. He wished he'd brought a torch. He lay down on his stomach and reached down into the black void. There was something there. Wooden. A ladder?

'Colm, can you hear me?' he asked.

There was no reply.

'Don't worry. I'll be with you in a minute,' he said.

Without thinking, without wasting another moment, he began to climb down the ladder until the darkness wrapped around him like a cloak.

·◆·

Colm had almost reached the bedroom door when he noticed the wet, muddy footprints on the carpet. The Brute must have been out for a walk in the rain, he thought with a smile. Serves him right if he got a good soaking.

The door was unlocked. He went in, but didn't find The Brute lying on the bed watching television as he'd expected. Was he in the bathroom again? Maybe he was sick after all. He knocked on the bathroom door a couple of times, but there was no answer.

'Michael, are you in there?' he asked.

Still nothing. That'd be just like The Brute. He wasn't even polite enough to reply.

'All right, have it your way,' he said.

He sat down by the dresser, picked up his book and began to read. The words didn't blur together this time. He smiled with relief. He was glad the whole worry of *The Book of Dread* had lifted, but there was still something nagging at him. Unanswered questions. He didn't like this hotel. Not one little bit. He couldn't wait until morning when they'd be far away from here. He never wanted to come back to this place, not as long as he lived.

He turned his attention back to the book. Reading would take his mind off things, although he was glad he wasn't reading a horror novel.

He'd only read half a page when he saw the white folded piece of paper on the ground. It looked like someone had slipped it under the door. Had he walked past it when he'd come in? Then he remembered the muddy footprints in the corridor. Probably some trick of The Brute's. He'd bend down to pick it up and his cousin would kick him up the bum. But he still hadn't heard any sound from the bathroom.

He marked the page in his book, placed it on the dresser, then went over and picked up the piece of paper. He opened it up and read:

Leave the hotel now
Before it's too late

Ten

his name was Paddy but everyone called him Bullkiller. Because that's what he told them to call him. It's never cool to give yourself a nickname, but nobody was brave enough to point this out to Paddy. He was huge and unpleasant, both in features and personality. He had spent twenty years on the Alaskan pipelines, one of the hardest jobs in a frozen climate, working alongside some of the toughest men that had ever existed. And even they were afraid of him.

It was a Thursday night and on Thursdays Paddy had a routine he had followed ever since he'd returned to Ireland. First he'd have a dinner of two steaks and chips, then he'd go to his local pub, drink a few pints and finally he'd pick a fight with someone. It didn't take much – if you looked at him the wrong way or made some innocent remark that he pretended to be offended by, then you'd be the one he'd choose – and less than two minutes later it would all be over. As a result most people avoided the pub on Thursday nights, but tonight Paddy the Bullkiller was happy. A stranger sat at one of the tables quietly reading a newspaper and drinking a cup of coffee.

Paddy got up from his seat at the bar. This took some time because his bulk made him a slow mover. The barman realised what he was up to and ducked down behind the dishwasher for safety as Paddy ambled to the man's table.

His large frame cast a shadow across the newspaper, but the man at the table didn't look up. Paddy scratched his chin and thought about the best way to start the fight. Maybe tonight he'd just give the man a shove and take it from there. He'd had a long day at work and wasn't in the mood for making conversation. But before he had the chance to do anything the man did something unexpected – he took off his watch and placed it carefully on the table.

Paddy was confused. To be honest, it didn't take much to confuse him, but he didn't understand what the man was doing. He was about to ask when the man spoke, as if anticipating the question.

'The watch is very expensive.' He picked it up and held it out in front of him so that Paddy could get a better look at it. 'Those are real diamonds where the numbers twelve and six should be. Do you like it?'

Paddy began to feel uneasy. This wasn't going the way he'd planned. Usually at this point his victim would be lying on the ground whining about his nose or his teeth or his fingers, not telling him about a watch.

'I asked you a question. Do you like it?'

Paddy the Bullkiller nodded. 'Very nice,' he mumbled. What was wrong with him? He was finding it difficult to speak. There was something about this man that frightened him and he didn't know why. The man was small. Weedy too. There was no obvious reason to be afraid of him. But he was. He wished he'd stayed sitting by the bar drinking his beer.

'Do you know why I took off my expensive watch?' asked the man, placing it on the table once more.

Paddy shook his head.

'I took it off so that it won't get damaged when I break you into tiny pieces.'

The man got to his feet. His head barely reached Paddy's chest, but Bullkiller took a step backwards.

'Don't break me into tiny pieces,' he said in a voice so small it could have been a little girl speaking.

'Say please,' said the man.

'Please don't break me into tiny little pieces,' Paddy squeaked.

The man sat down, put on his watch and began reading the newspaper again.

'Leave now,' he said to Paddy without even looking at him.

Paddy the Bullkiller didn't need to be told twice. He turned on his heel and left the pub immediately, not even stopping to collect his coat or the wallet he'd left lying on the bar.

The rat-faced little man nodded to the barman. 'Another coffee,' he said.

'Yes, sir,' said the barman who'd never called anyone sir in his life before.

Eleven

Colm heard his mother before he saw her. She was singing as she walked down the hotel corridor. He stuffed the paper into his pocket before she entered the room.

'Hi love, everything OK?' she asked.

Colm half-expected her to kiss him again, but she didn't. No point doing it unless there were crowds of people to witness his humiliation.

'Everything's fine, Mam,' he answered.

'That was the nicest meal I've had in ten years,' she said. 'We're so lucky to have found this hotel.'

Colm felt like laughing. If she thought this was good luck then he'd hate to think what bad luck must be like.

'How's Michael?' she asked.

'Fine. I think. He's still in the bathroom.'

'Still?'

She banged on the bathroom door.

'Michael, are you all right in there?'

No answer.

'Michael, it's me, Auntie Mary. Look there's nothing to be embarrassed about. We've all been … er … sick at some time in our lives. Just let me know you're OK, hon.'

Still nothing.

'How long has he been in there, Colm?'

'I dunno. An hour.'

'An hour?'

Lines appeared on her forehead. A sure sign she was worried. She banged on the door again. 'Michael, if you don't answer me in the next thirty seconds then I'm going to come in.'

Five seconds later she opened the door and stormed in. Colm cringed. This could be unpleasant. When she emerged from the bathroom all the colour had drained from her face.

'What's wrong?' he asked. It didn't look good.

'He's not there,' she said. Her lips went dry and thin. 'Where is he, Colm?'

'I don't know. I thought he was in there.'

'This is serious, young man.'

Oh no. 'Young man' meant trouble. Big trouble.

'I-I-I don't know, Mam,' he stammered.

'I'll put it this way, Colm. If you don't tell me what's going on in the next ten seconds, then you're grounded until your thirteenth birthday. And that'll only be the start of your punishment. I'm too angry right now to even begin to think up any others, but believe me, I will. So, what's it going to be?'

·◆·

Within five minutes Colm's bedroom was a flurry of activity. His dad arrived along with Mrs McMahon, Lauryn, Lauryn's mother Marie – who was as beautiful as her daughter, but looked as if she hadn't slept in weeks – as well as the porter-waiter, the only one of the staff who was still in the hotel. There were plenty of raised voices and pointed fingers until eventually Colm's dad managed to calm them down with a few well chosen words.

'SHUT UP,' he roared.

Six faces turned towards him.

'We can argue and point fingers later. Now we need to find Michael. Agreed?'

There were a few nods and muttered words.

'Right. Lauryn, is it?'

Lauryn stepped forward. Colm noticed that her shoes were covered in mud.

'Colm seems to think that you and Michael might have arranged to meet up. Is that true?'

'Yes, but I forgot about it. Sorry,' Lauryn said.

'You forgot? How could you forget?' Colm's mother asked angrily.

'She has a lot on her mind,' said Marie, her accent a strange mix of Irish and American.

'I've a lot on my mind. My nephew is missing,' Colm's mother replied.

'Easy, Mary,' said Colm's father.

'Don't easy me,' said his mother. 'Anything could have happened to him.'

'But losing our heads won't do us any good. Not now. Where were you going to meet him, Lauryn?'

'I was supposed to call to his room. Here.'

'Where did you go instead?'

Lauryn looked to her mother, as if checking that it was all right to answer. Marie smiled which Lauryn took as a yes.

'I went into the woods,' she said.

'What would a young girl like you want to go into the woods at that time of night for?' Colm's mother asked.

'That's got nothing to do with you,' said Mrs McMahon.

'It does when my nephew's missing.'

'No. It doesn't,' Mrs McMahon said firmly.

Colm's father ignored the conversation.

'Do you think it's possible that he went into the woods by himself?' he asked.

Lauryn was surprised at the suggestion. As if it had never occurred to her.

'I suppose so. I didn't see anyone else when I was in there,' she said.

'Right. This is what we're going to do,' Colm's father said. 'You, what's your name?'

'Mr Jenkins,' said the porter-waiter haughtily.

'Mr Jenkins and me are going to go into the woods and look for him.'

'Those woods are much larger than they look,' said Mrs McMahon.

'Well, we're still going to go. Mrs McMahon, Lauryn and Lauryn's mother – I'm afraid I've forgotten your name.'

'Marie.'

'You three know this hotel inside out, I bet. I'd like you to check it from top to bottom.'

'No problem,' Lauryn said.

'Colm and Mary, you stay here in case he comes back.' He took his mobile phone from his pocket. 'If you haven't heard from me in thirty minutes, ring the Gardaí.'

'Mr Sweeney,' said Jenkins.

'What?'

'I'd like to make a request,' he said.

'If this is about money, I've already given you twenty euro.'

'No, sir. If you would like to turn slightly to your left you might find the young gentleman that appears to be the cause of all this concern.'

The Brute stood at the door.

'Hiya. What's going on?' he asked.

·◆·

It took some time for everything and everybody to calm down, but finally there was some sort of order. The Brute looked exhausted and bedraggled. He was filthy and soaked and his clothes were torn, but he was in good health. He was also in good spirits. Even when his aunt had stopped hugging him and started to give out.

'You had me at death's door with the worry.'

'Sorry, Auntie Mary.'

'How dare you pretend to be sick and then sneak off like that.'

'Sorry, Auntie Mary.'

'Anything could have happened to you and if it did what would I tell your poor mother? She'd be heartbroken.'

'Sorry, Auntie Mary.'

Eventually she ran out of complaints and gave him another hug, not even caring that she was ruining her own clothes. They made him drink cups of hot, sweet tea – for the shock they said – and Mrs McMahon told them how once, long ago, a man went into the woods and never came out again.

'That's why I always warn the guests to stick to the path,' she said.

Lauryn apologised to The Brute for not meeting up with him as they'd planned, but he didn't seem to mind. He just laughed – laughed! – and said it didn't matter. He'd had a great adventure. He even started talking about how much he loved the hotel, which seemed to please Mrs McMahon, and he would have rambled on for even longer if Colm's mother hadn't told him to have a shower and change his clothes before he caught pneumonia.

They all began to drift out of the room then, glad that the drama was over. Colm's mother told him to keep an eye on The Brute and if he was ill during the night to call her immediately. He promised he would.

He walked his parents out to the corridor and when they were safely in their room he ran after Lauryn. He caught up with her at the bottom of the stairs.

'What's up?' she asked. 'Is your cousin all right?'

'He's fine,' said Colm. 'I just wanted to give you this. You left it in our room.'

He took the folded piece of white paper from his pocket and handed it to her, watching for her reaction. Nothing. She just looked at it.

'What's this supposed to be?' she asked. 'Some kind of joke?'

'You tell me,' Colm said bravely.

'I've never seen this before in my life,' she said.

'Except when you wrote it,' he replied.

Lauryn flinched. It lasted less than a second, but it was enough to convince Colm that she'd written the note.

'Why did you do that? Is it just another stupid joke, like *The Book of Dread*?' he asked. His angry tone surprised him. He was usually the quietest one in any room.

'I told you I didn't write it,' she said. Her lips were set tight as if she was angry at the accusation.

'OK,' Colm said calmly. He took the paper from her, folded it neatly and put it in the back pocket of his jeans. 'If you didn't write it then someone in this hotel did. I'll show it to my parents and see what they think. After what's just happened with The B ... Michael, I don't think my mam will be too happy. She'll probably ring the Gardaí.'

He started back up the stairs. He'd only reached the third step when Lauryn called after him.

'Wait,' she said.

·•◆•·

The Brute was surprised to find the room was empty when he'd finished his shower. Two showers in one day. He wouldn't have to wash for a week. He dried his hair with a towel and then tried to brush it into shape. No matter what he did, it didn't look good. Normally, he'd have spent ages trying to style it with American wax, but he was too tired to do that now.

He lay down on the bed. All of a sudden he was exhausted. Funny. Only a few minutes before he'd been in great form. Happier than he'd been in years and now it had worn off him. Just like that. Maybe he was coming down with something.

His eyes began to close. He was on the edge of sleep. Images kept popping into his head. The woods. Had he really been there? It seemed like a dream now that he was safely back in the hotel room. The trapdoor. That was real, wasn't it? He'd climbed down the ladder. He could almost feel his feet on the wooden steps that had splintered and cracked. They were rotten from age. It was dark down there. Pitch black. He couldn't see anything at first. Even when his eyes had adjusted to the darkness things hadn't been any clearer. But he remembered the smell. That horrible musty smell. That was it. It was like he was still there. The spongy earth beneath his feet. The rotten stench. The cold touch of granite.

What happened then? The hissing. He'd thought it was a snake at first until he realised that was a stupid thought.

He knew it had to be something else. Something trying to breathe. As if every breath was a struggle. Something ancient. He'd walked towards it. Why was he even there? He'd been looking for Colm. That was it. But as soon as he knew Colm wasn't down there why hadn't he just climbed up the ladder and run away?

Because he couldn't. The thing, that vile old thing, was calling to him. That was when he realised that the voice he'd heard hadn't been coming from under the ground. It had been inside his head all the time. The thing was communicating with him. No, not communicating. What was it? Commanding him.

He'd gone towards it without even stopping to think why. He'd reached out and felt its robes. Foul smelling and damp. What then? Now he remembered. The eye. One blood-red eye.

He woke up with a start. His forehead was covered with sweat. He wiped it off and sat up. That was one bad dream, he thought. He got up from the bed. His jacket was hanging on the back of the chair. Water dripped from it on to the floor forming a little pool on the carpet. His favourite jacket ruined. He sighed. He wished he was at home. In his own bed.

He inspected the arm of the jacket. Even if his mother sewed it up it'd look manky. And she wouldn't buy him another one. He knew she'd just bang on about how expensive jackets were and how money didn't grow on trees and stuff like that. She'd had enough money to go to Lanzarote though. Maybe he'd say that to her if she made a fuss.

There was something in the jacket pocket. It all came back to him in a flash. It wasn't a bad dream. He had been there. Under the ground. With that thing. And he'd taken something. Even though every part of him had screamed to leave it behind, he'd taken it.

He shook the jacket until the object came loose and rolled onto the floor. It gleamed in the light.

The Brute's stomach lurched. He thought he was going to be sick. He slumped to the floor. What had he done?

Twelve

Colm used to love libraries. He loved finding books he had never heard of before and taking them home like some secret treasure. He was beginning to change his mind. Every time he'd visited this library bad things had happened.

'When are you going to tell me?' he asked.

'Just a couple more minutes,' Lauryn replied.

'What are we waiting for?'

'Please be quiet,' she said.

Lauryn got out of her chair and began pacing up and down.

'Look, if you're not going to tell me, then I'm leaving,' Colm said.

The library door creaked open and a man appeared. He had long dark hair and a beard, and he wore a tweed jacket over a check shirt and a pair of jeans. He looked about forty years old. He held a cigarette between his yellow, stained fingers, the smoke curling up towards the ceiling.

'Hello, Colm,' he said.

Colm had never seen the man before in his life, so he assumed Lauryn must have told him his name.

'Hi,' he replied.

The man stood in front of him and Colm had to arch his neck just to look him in the face. The man was tall. Very tall. Thin too – the fingers that wrapped themselves around the cigarette were long and bony.

'My name is Peter Drake,' said the man in a deep, rich voice. 'There's no need to be afraid.'

Colm hadn't been afraid. Not until the man had mentioned it. Now, he began to wonder if there was yet another thing to worry about.

'Professor Drake will explain everything,' Lauryn said.

'Actually, Lauryn, I won't. We don't have time for explanations,' Drake replied.

'What's going on?' Colm asked.

'Colm, I know you don't know me, but I'm going to ask you to go out on a limb and trust me,' Drake said.

In Colm's experience when someone asked you to trust them it usually meant you shouldn't. The Brute was always saying things like that: 'Trust me, this won't hurt a bit.' But it did. It always hurt.

'Can you come with me, please,' Drake said. It was more of a demand than a question. It wasn't the words he used, it was the way he said it.

'Where?' he asked.

'Somewhere safe.'

'I'm fine here,' Colm said. He looked around. No exits other than the door and Drake was blocking that. He wasn't making a big deal of it, he was acting all casual, but Colm knew by the way the man shifted the weight from his left foot to his right that he was preparing himself in case Colm made a run for it. What did they want with him?

His mouth went dry. He would have killed for a glass of water.

Lauryn sensed his discomfort.

'It's all right, Colm. Just do as he says.'

She said it like she was on his side. If she really was then why had she told him that lie about *The Book of Dread*? Why had she slipped the note under the door? Why had she let The Brute go into the woods?

In the past he would have just done what he was told, but if he'd learned one thing from The Brute, it was to act on his instincts. No point waiting. Go now.

'OK, I'll go with you,' he said.

The man had heard what he'd wanted to hear. His

shoulders relaxed. Just for a split second. But it was enough time for Colm to make his move.

He sprinted to the man's left. Drake's jaw dropped and the cigarette fell from his lips. Colm had caught him off guard. But the tall, thin man was quick, quicker than he looked. His long arm snaked out.

Not far enough.

Colm dodged to man's right. Sold him a dummy. The man lurched in the wrong direction. Too late to catch him.

The door was only three yards away. Already he was thinking ahead. Grab the key on the way out. Lock them in the room. He'd have to be fast.

The blur of movement came from his right. He saw it out of the corner of his eye.

Lauryn diving through the air.

Her shoulder hit him in the fleshy part of his stomach. Colm heard a soft sound.

Oomph.

Then he felt the pain surge through his body and realised he was the one who'd made the noise.

They crashed to the floor in a heap of arms and legs. Before Colm had the chance to untangle himself from the mess Drake had grabbed him by the collar. He picked him up as if he weighed nothing at all and flung him onto the armchair.

'We tried to be nice about this,' Drake snarled.

'What are you doing? Are you crazy?' Colm shouted.

'It's not what it looks like,' Lauryn said. She seemed sad. Almost ashamed.

'It looks like you're trying to take me prisoner,' Colm said. 'Can I leave?'

She shook her head.

'Then it's exactly what it looks like,' he said.

'We'll put him with the others,' Drake said. He took a length of blue rope from his pocket.

'What others?' Colm asked, but he knew the answer before he'd even finished the question. His mam and dad. 'You two are nuts.'

'Your opinion on this matter is entirely redundant,' Drake said. 'Put your hands out. Like this.'

Drake held his arms out in front of him and pressed his wrists together.

'What if I say no?' Colm asked.

'Then it'll hurt more when I tie you up.'

How did he know Drake was going to say that?

Colm wasn't sure what to do. He thought of making a break for it again, but they'd be expecting it this time. The element of surprise was gone. Reluctantly, he put his hands out.

Drake tied the knot tightly, then triple checked it wasn't

going to loosen. Typical professor. Leaving nothing to chance. The rope was rough and scratchy and it tore at Colm's wrists. Not much hope of getting out of this, he thought.

'Stand up,' Drake said.

Colm got to his feet. It wasn't easy with his hands tied up. He shuffled about in the chair until Drake lost his patience, grabbed the rope and hauled him up.

'Where are you taking me?' he asked. Great question Colm, he thought.

'Somewhere safe,' Drake replied giving him a shove in the back.

Colm took a few steps forward. It was weird walking with his hands tied up. It was weird just being tied up. He caught Lauryn's eye, but she quickly looked away. Definitely feeling guilty, he decided.

As she held the door open twin beams of light swept through the room. Headlights outside. They heard the crunch of tyres on gravel as the car turned in the courtyard.

'Stay here with the boy. Don't let him out of your sight,' said Drake hurrying towards the front door of the hotel.

Lauryn shut the library door and switched off the light. Moonlight streamed through the only window without curtains, the one at the opposite end of the room to the door. The light cast strange shadows on the walls like monsters from a nightmare. At any other time in his life this would have unnerved him, but shadows were the least of his worries now.

'Lauryn, can I tell you something?'

'No. Not now.'

Colm ignored her. He wanted to say something smart. Something cutting. Something witty like James Bond would say if he was in the same situation.

'You're not going to get away with this,' he said.

Good one Colm, he thought, that was worth the wait.

Drake peered through the door viewer as the car came to a stop in front of the hotel. Two people got out. A man and a woman. Cedric Murphy and Kate Finkle.

·◆·

A grey mist shrouded the hotel in a ghostly gloom. Kate shivered. And not just because it was cold. At least the rain has stopped, she thought. She was sitting on the bonnet of the Ford Focus puffing on a cigar when Cedric returned.

'There's a car parked round the back of the hotel. A navy BMW. The registration matches the one Mark gave us,' he said with a smile.

'Great. Can we go now?' Kate said. 'This place is giving me the creeps.'

'It's a hotel, Kate. How can a hotel give you the creeps?'

'I dunno, all this mist and trees and stuff. Something's not right. I can feel it in my waters.'

'There's a pleasant thought,' he said.

'Believe me, Ced, humans aren't meant to live in the countryside. Not any more. Give me the city and crowds of people any day. So, can we go?'

'Not yet. I'm not ringing our client until I've made a positive ID. If I send him on a wild goose chase who knows what he might do to me.'

'You want to meet the man in the photo?'

'You got it in one.'

They crossed the courtyard. Somewhere in the woods an owl hooted. Kate almost leaped into Cedric's arms.

'What was that?' she asked in a tiny voice.

'Only the most terrifying creature ever known to man,' Cedric said.

Kate's eyes opened wide.

'It's an owl, Kate. Just an owl. I thought you liked animals.'

'Owls are birds, not animals. I like cats and goldfish, Ced. Things you can keep indoors. You can't keep an owl indoors.'

'You could try.' Cedric turned the brass door knob. Nothing happened. 'That's strange,' he said. 'It's locked. Why would a hotel be locked up at night?'

He banged on the door three times with the heel of his fist.

'Maybe the hotel staff are worried that strange creatures will sneak in and savage them. You know, I saw this film once – *The Birds* – where all the birds turned evil and started attacking ...'

The door opened a little and Peter Drake poked his head out.

'Can I help you?' he asked coldly.

Cedric pushed past him into the lobby, much to Drake's annoyance. 'No point in chatting out on the steps. It's freezing out there,' Cedric said.

'The hotel's closed,' Drake said. 'For renovations.'

'That's a shame. We were looking for a room for the night.'

Drake looked at his watch. 'It's gone midnight.'

'Well, we were looking for a room for the morning then. We've been travelling for hours.'

'As I said – we're closed. I'm afraid I'll have to ask you to leave,' Drake said.

'No problem. Could you recommend somewhere else to stay?'

Kate looked around the lobby. Seemed like a nice hotel. If you liked old places. She half heard Cedric ask the man for a phone book to look up numbers for bed and breakfasts. What was he playing at? The tall man was the one they were looking for, wasn't he? She glanced at the paintings on the wall. Wow, some ugly old geezers up there. Wouldn't have liked to have hung around with them. One-way ticket to boredom city and ... whoa, who was that guy with the red eyes? Kate was glad she wasn't around in his time. He looked mad and dangerous. She walked up a few steps to get a closer look at the painting. Yup, definite bad guy.

'Excuse me. Where do you think you're going?'

Kate turned around. Drake and Cedric were looking up at her.

'Yes, I'm talking to you. This is a private dwelling and you're trespassing. Please leave immediately,' Drake snarled.

'Sorry. Just looking at the paintings,' Kate said. 'They're beautiful. They take my breath away,' she lied.

'You take my breath away, darling,' Cedric said with a smirk. 'Why don't you wait for me in the car while I get the telephone numbers from Mr ...'

'Smith,' said Drake.

'Smith. Very popular name,' Cedric replied.

·•◆•·

Colm could hear the voices outside and wondered if he should shout for help. Lauryn seemed to read his mind.

'Don't say a word, Colm,' she warned him.

He took a step towards the door. Lauryn immediately stood in front of it, blocking him.

When he heard the front door slam he ran towards her. She put her hands out to stop him, but he turned on his heel – not easy with his hands tied up – and ran in the opposite direction. He looked like a toddler taking his first steps.

'You can't get out that way,' Lauryn said.

But he wasn't looking for a way out.

He darted towards the window. She saw what he was going to do.

'Don't,' she said.

He tried to push through the heavy velvet curtains, but got caught up in them. They wrapped themselves around his head and for a moment he thought he was going to suffocate. Lauryn pulled at his shirt.

'Get away from there,' she whispered, not daring to speak out loud in case she was heard in the lobby.

He let her think he'd given up. She dragged him back, but when he didn't put up any resistance her grip on him slackened. He took the chance and lunged forward at the window. His face slapped against the glass.

The large woman outside by the car must have got a fright because she nearly jumped out of her skin when she heard whack of his cheekbone on the window pane. He only had a second. He mouthed a single word. Help.

He didn't know if the woman had seen him or not. He didn't have the time to check. Lauryn grabbed him by the waist and spun him around. Her eyes blazed with anger.

'That was a stupid thing to do,' she said in a furious whisper.

'What? Trying to escape? Yeah, I don't know what I was thinking,' Colm replied.

'This isn't the time for sarcasm. This is serious.'

He held up his hands to show her the rope that bound them.

'You think I don't know that,' he said.

·◆·

'OK, I'd better head off. Still got a bit of travelling to do,' said Cedric making his way to the door. 'Thanks for your help, Mr Sm ...'

Drake slammed the door shut in his face.

'Ced?'

'Not now, Kate. We'll talk in the car. Just act like we're a normal couple. He's watching us through the door viewer,' Cedric whispered, taking her hand.

They got into the car and Cedric started it up. He revved the engine.

'Ced. Did you see …'

'Wait until we're out of here. Caution is our watch-word.'

They headed out the long driveway and the car turned on to the main road.

'Cedric?'

'A few more seconds, Kate.'

When they were about half a mile away from the hotel Cedric banged the steering wheel with his fist. He beeped the car horn joyfully. He may even have shouted 'Yeehaw'. A huge smile spread across his pudgy features.

'That was him all right. The man we're looking for. I can't believe it. We did it. You know, I was feeling sorry for the tall guy and whatever trouble he was in until I met him. Now I feel nothing. He's a nasty piece of work. He deserves whatever's coming to him. I feel relieved. The last few hours have been so stressful.'

'There was a boy in there,' Kate said.

'What?'

'A boy. At the window. I saw him when I was waiting for you by the car. I think he's in trouble. He asked me to help him.'

'I didn't hear anyone shout for help. I would have heard it if I was only in the next room,' Cedric said.

'He didn't say it out loud. He mouthed it to me.'

'Well, in all fairness, Kate, you're not a trained lip reader. Maybe he was saying something else. Like "whelp".'

'Whelp?'

'It's a word. Look it up in the dictionary.'

'Don't play me for a fool, Cedric Murphy.'

'He was probably just playing a stupid game. You know how children are, especially these days – nasty, spiteful little gits.'

'We have to go back and help that boy. We can't just leave him there. You know that.'

Cedric sighed. 'I wish we could, Kate. But we can't. If we interfere with The Ghost's work, then you know what'll happen to us.'

As if on cue, Cedric's mobile phone rang.

'Hand me that, Kate.'

She slapped the phone into his hand.

'You know it's illegal to talk on the phone while driving.'

'We've already done plenty of illegal things today. One more won't make a difference,' Cedric said, but he still indicated and pulled the car over to the side of the road before he answered the call.

'Hello. Yes, I'm aware that my time is now up, but I have good news for you. I have found the man you were looking for.'

He gave the rat-faced little man instructions on how to get to the Red House Hotel.

'Before you go, I just want to clarify one thing – my work is finished now, right? Thank you sir.'

He hung up.

'Sir? You called him sir,' Kate mocked.

'If you'd met him you'd call him sir too,' Cedric said. 'Anyway, the money will be in my bank account in the morning and he said that we're in the clear. As far as he's concerned our work is done and we never have to worry about him again.'

'And what about the boy? Are you worried about him?'

'Kate, you're beginning to annoy me.'

'And you've been annoying me for years, but I've put up with it, so surely you can give me a minute of your precious time.'

Cedric nodded. 'Go on.'

'Couldn't we just go back and get the boy out of there before Mr Smith arrives?'

'Too risky. And for all we know our client may want to talk to the boy.'

'OK, let's just ring the Gardaí then. Anonymously. They could take care of it and no one would ever know that we were involved.'

'*He* would. Come on, Kate, do you really think he got to where he is by being stupid? If the Gardaí turned up he'd know it was us who tipped them off and then he'd come after us. I'm sorry. You know in any other circumstances I'd love to help, but I can't do that now. That's my final word on the matter. The boy is on his own.'

Thirteen

Lauryn led Colm up the stairs, Drake just behind her. It was difficult to climb the steps with his hands bound and he stumbled once or twice, but Lauryn was there to steady him.

'It'll be OK,' she said.

'It will be OK if you let us all go,' Colm replied.

'We can't do that,' Drake said. 'It's for your own good.'

Colm doubted that.

They arrived at number thirteen. Drake took a bunch of keys from his pocket. Colm knew the door was unlocked, but he wasn't going to tell them that. He was being petty and he liked it.

He decided to take a chance. Call their bluff. 'Do you really think you'll find it?' he asked.

Drake seemed surprised. 'Find what?'

'The Lazarus Key. That's what you're looking for, isn't it?'

'He must have read the book,' Lauryn said to Drake.

'I thought I told you to hide it.' Drake sounded more weary than angry.

'I didn't think we needed to when the hotel was closed. Anyway, I told him it was cursed. I didn't think he'd be brave enough to look at it if he thought bad things would happen,' Lauryn said.

She'd underestimated him.

'Maybe he's not afraid of curses,' Drake said, opening the door. 'Lauryn, take off the rope.'

'Are you sure it's safe?' she asked.

'If he doesn't go quietly into the room there'll be consequences. You don't want there to be consequences, do you?'

Colm didn't bother to reply. That'd show him. Unless it was a rhetorical question.

The knot was tied very tightly and it took Lauryn a few minutes to loosen the rope. Drake kept making impatient noises and urging her to hurry up. Her cheeks reddened and Colm saw that she was on the verge of losing her temper. He wondered if there was a way he could use that against them, but she finished untying the knot before he'd even begun to think of a plan.

Drake shoved him into the room.

'Don't try to leave. Just sit there quietly and in a few hours this will all be over,' he said.

Colm wasn't sure what he meant by that. What would be over? Was he going to steal the Lazarus Key and then just let them go? He didn't think so. Somehow he knew that things weren't going to work out that easily.

Drake slammed the door, locking it after him. Colm heard the click as the key turned. His heart sank.

'Oooooooohhh.'

The sound came from between the two beds. The Brute was lying on the ground, his face a sickly colour.

'Are you OK?' Colm asked. Stupid question. He looked like death warmed up.

The Brute slowly opened his eyes. 'Colm?'

Not Dogpoo or Eighth Dwarf or Piggy Piggy Four Eyes. He'd called him Colm. That wasn't a good sign.

'What's wrong?'

'Water. I need water.' He propped himself up against the side of the bed. It took him ages, as if all the energy had drained out of him.

Colm ran to the bathroom, filled a glass and took it to his cousin.

He held the glass out but The Brute didn't reach for it. Colm saw that he was trying to focus on it, but he couldn't keep his eyes open and his head kept flopping from side to side.

Colm knelt down beside him, held him by the back of the neck and pressed the glass to his lips. He gulped back the water as if he hadn't had a drink in days. Streams of it poured down the sides of his mouth and onto his shirt.

Colm refilled the glass and set it down on the floor beside The Brute. He didn't know what to do. He must have got sick from being stuck out in the rain when he went looking for Lauryn, he thought. That girl was making him really angry. What did she have against him and his family? He didn't care if she went looking for the Lazarus Key. The tall, thin man and her could look for a hundred keys as far as he was concerned. He wasn't going to try to stop them. There was no reason for her to have locked them up like this. He wanted to kick something. Now he knew how The Brute felt most of the time.

He calmed himself down. Being angry wouldn't help him. Not now. He needed to think. First, he had to make sure The Brute was OK. He'd put him on the bed. Could he lift him? He was about to find out.

He put his hands under The Brute's armpits.

'Michael, I'm going to lift you on the count of three,' he said.

The Brute didn't seem to register what he was saying.

'One. Two. Three.'

He heaved with all his might, but it was no good. He weighed a ton. There was no chance of him lifting him on to the bed. But he had to.

'OK, this time I'm going to save some energy. I'm only going to count to one,' he said.

He took a few deep breaths and tried again. The first time he tried The Brute didn't budge an inch, the second time, he did. Literally an inch. Colm dropped him back to the ground and something fell from The Brute's hand.

'The room key,' Colm thought. Joy and hope exchanged high-fives in his mind. The man who called himself Drake had had a large bunch of keys in his hand. They must be the master keys of the hotel. But he had forgotten something – The Brute had the room key Mrs McMahon had given to him. Some professor he was.

He bent down to pick it up only to find it wasn't the room key at all. It was a diamond, one-tenth the size of his hand. It looked like there was something inside it. How did that get in there? He lifted it up to the light to get a better look at it.

He was right. There was something in there. No bigger than his thumbnail. It was a tiny skull.

'At least it's not the Lazarus Key,' he said, remembering the story from *The Book of Dread*.

'No,' said The Brute.

Colm didn't hear him. Was there something in the book about a skull with a diamond inside it? There was a mention of a tattoo, wasn't there? He stared at the diamond. How had they even managed to put a tiny skull in there? Maybe it was some technique, like the way they put a ship in a bottle. He wondered what The Brute was doing with it.

'NO,' shouted The Brute, his face a mask of terror.

He heard him this time.

'What is it? What's wrong, Michael?' Colm said, trying to keep the worry out of his voice. The Brute needed a doctor. He looked dreadful.

'It's coming for me,' he said.

'What's coming for you?' Colm asked.

'The creature,' said The Brute.

·◆·

'Are you sure you don't remember?' Drake asked.

'I'd tell you if I could. Do you think I want to be part of this mess? You're going to ruin my reputation. Closing the hotel. Kidnapping guests. Ghosts on the prowl. I'll be destroyed,' said Mrs McMahon.

'Could you please look at the map again? Anything you can think of, no matter how small or insignificant it might be,' he said.

The map of the Red House estate was spread across the stainless steel kitchen counter. Pots and pans of all shapes and sizes were stacked up neatly by the sink. Steam rose from the kettle as it came to the boil.

'Turn that thing off,' Drake said.

'Don't be telling me what to do in my own hotel,' Mrs McMahon said, using glare number fourteen from her collection of vicious looks.

Drake lit up a cigarette as Marie and Lauryn came into the kitchen. Lauryn hopped onto the countertop, her legs dangling over the edge.

'Don't be sitting there like some useless article, Lauryn. Make us all a cup of tea.'

Drake grabbed a saucepan and flung it against the wall. It clattered to the ground.

'There's no time for tea,' he roared.

Mrs McMahon had faced tougher men than him and she wasn't about to back down.

'But there's time to smoke a cigarette, is there?' she asked.

Drake lit another cigarette even though he hadn't finished the first one. He tapped his watch.

'We don't have time for all of this. We have to find the Key and get out of here,' he said, thoroughly frustrated by Mrs McMahon's stubbornness.

'Explain it to me again. I want to understand it fully,' she said.

'What good will that do, Mam?' Marie asked.

'Because if you let me know exactly what you're looking

for,' said Mrs McMahon, 'I might be able to tell you where you can find it.'

·◆·

Colm had searched the room three times before he thought of looking in the bathroom. It was there all right, just where he'd least expected it to be. The Brute's fleece, still soaking wet, was thrown in the bath. Colm couldn't even imagine what had led his cousin to put it there, but he was acting so strangely – because of an illness, because of something else? – that he knew he should have thought of looking there earlier.

He put his hand in the wet, slimy pocket. Nothing other than a handkerchief – and it had been used. Great. The room key was in the other pocket.

He checked on The Brute. Colour was coming back to his cheeks. That was good. He looked even more frightened than he had earlier. That wasn't so good.

He pocketed the diamond, not really knowing why. Maybe it would be of some use later.

'I'll be back in a minute,' he said to The Brute.

'Don't leave me, Colm. Please. I don't want to be alone when it comes for me,' he replied.

Colm didn't want to be there when it came for him either. But he would. No matter how much he disliked The

Brute, and he disliked him a lot, he couldn't let him face the creature alone. You don't desert family in their hour of need, he told himself.

'I'll only be five minutes,' he said. 'I'm just going to go down to reception. There's a phone there. I'll ring the guards and I'll come straight back up.'

'Promise,' The Brute said in a thin, reedy voice.

'I promise.'

He hated seeing his cousin like that, all weak and scared. He hoped that The Brute was just delirious from some bug or illness he'd picked up, but as soon as he'd mentioned the creature he knew, he just knew, that *The Book of Dread* wasn't some creepy story. It was very real.

He thought back to when The Brute had come back from his trip to the woods. He'd been happy. Far too happy for someone whose moods were limited to grumpy, very grumpy and pure rage. The man who'd written the book had said he was happy too. Just for a short while. And then he'd said the sickness followed. Colm wasn't a doctor, but even he could see that his cousin wasn't an advertisement for good health.

The last words the man had written were something about how the creature was coming for him. He knew it before it had arrived. Just the way The Brute knew it now. The Brute had held the Lazarus Key. He wanted to ask him about it, but there wasn't a chance of getting him to say anything sensible when he was in this state.

Colm reviewed the situation. Here he was in a place he didn't like. With his parents locked away somewhere. With his older cousin sick. With a creature on the loose. And it was dark. And cold. And he didn't have a weapon. Well, he supposed, things couldn't get much worse.

Of course, he was wrong.

Fourteen

Colm put the key in the lock. For one horrible moment he thought it wasn't going to turn, but it was just rusty and with a bit of effort he managed to open it. He pressed his fingers to his lips letting The Brute know he should be quiet, but there was no need. His cousin just sat silently on the ground, his head resting on the edge of the bed.

He eased the door open and snuck out into the corridor. The carpet softened his footsteps and he was as quiet as a mouse. He reached the stairs and peered through the banisters. He couldn't see all of the lobby from up there, but it looked like the coast was clear and he wasn't going to waste any more time just waiting. He'd already done too much of that.

His heart was thumping as he crept down the stairs. With every step he took he expected the boards beneath the carpet to creak and for someone to come running, but the stairs didn't creak and nobody appeared. He walked past the paintings and glanced up at the strange portrait of the man with the scar and the long black hair. And the blood-red eyes.

That must be Hugh DeLancey-O'Brien, was his first thought. Well d'uh, was his second. He should have known that ages ago. There was something about this hotel that clouded the mind, stopped people thinking clearly. Either that or he wasn't as smart as he thought he was.

He stepped on to the tiled floor and looked around more carefully than he would if he was crossing a busy road. Still nobody around.

Fog slipped beneath the front door. He'd never seen that happen before. It didn't worry him too much, but it didn't make him feel good either.

The reception desk was only a few yards away. His heart beat even faster, if that was possible, and his legs wobbled like a giraffe on stilts. His brain told him to walk out the front door and keep walking out the driveway until he was far, far away from here. There was no doubt about it. He was afraid. And he couldn't shake it off.

That was the thing about fear. It grabbed you by the scruff of the neck and refused to let you go. He knew that. He didn't know that it also made you want to pay a visit to the bathroom. His stomach was churning. This was what his mother must have meant when she said she got butterflies in her stomach when she was nervous. If there were butterflies in his stomach then it felt like they were armour-plated and carrying machine-guns.

He had to block out the fear somehow. He wasn't going to be able to help anyone if he gave in to it. He closed his eyes for a second and tried to think calm thoughts. What made him calm? Watching the National Geographic channel. He tried to think of something he'd seen on a nature programme. Antelopes peacefully drinking at a waterhole. That'd do. But then another image popped into his head. Antelopes being chased by a bloodthirsty lion. Not helpful at all. He tried to get the image out of his head, but it just stuck there as if someone had superglued it to his brain.

He didn't have time for this. He tiptoed to the reception desk and slowly, carefully lifted the phone from its cradle. He listened for the dialling tone. Nothing. Zip. Nada. The line was as dead as a wasp in a jam jar of water.

Either Mrs McMahon hadn't paid her telephone bill or someone had disconnected the line. Why would they do that? Because they don't want someone – me – ringing the Gardaí, he thought. What now? His dad had a mobile, but he didn't know where that was. They'd probably taken it from him. Unless he'd left it in the car. He might have. He was always leaving his mobile lying around the place. It was worth a look.

Before he took a step towards the front door – a shroud of fog seemed to be building up around it – he heard the raised voices somewhere off to his right in the direction of the restaurant. Without thinking, he crossed the lobby and pushed through the swing doors.

Fifteen tables all neatly laid out. No diners. Creepy.

The voices were clearer now and he knew they were coming from the kitchen. He was sure of it. He inched his way through the restaurant. Halfway there he realised that if someone came out of the kitchen they'd see him straight away. There wouldn't be time to hide by ducking under one of the tablecloths. Stupid decision to come in here Colm, he said to himself. Should he keep going or turn back? When he overheard the words 'Lazarus Key' he decided to keep going.

The door to the kitchen was half-open. He pressed himself against the wall off to the side. Not a great place to find cover. He was too exposed, but if he wanted to find out what the argument was about this was where he needed to be. How come James Bond or Sherlock Holmes were never stuck like this? At least now he could hear the voices clearly. Drake and Mrs McMahon. Those two were definitely in there.

He slid down the wall, lowering himself to the ground until

he was on his haunches. Through the thin gap between the door hinges he could see a sliver of the kitchen. Legs dangled from a counter. The shoes looked like Lauryn's. That must be her, he thought. And there was her mother. She kept moving in and out of sight, a teapot in her hand.

'So are you going to tell me or not?' Mrs McMahon asked.

Drake lit up yet another cigarette.

'You know by now that your daughter works for me at the university in Philadelphia. Has done for years. She's my invaluable assistant and I couldn't do without her,' Drake said.

Mrs McMahon nodded. It was as grim as a nod can be.

'I'm a Professor of Antiquities. That means I'm involved with items or relics from ancient times,' Drake said.

'I know what antiquities means,' barked Mrs McMahon. 'Get to the point.'

'Seven days ago a man arrived in my office. Not the type of man you'd usually find in a university. He looked like a thug, didn't he, Marie?'

'Yes,' she said somewhat anxiously.

'He was carrying a briefcase. It looked out of place in his possession.'

Mrs McMahon sighed.

'I'm getting to it. Let me remind you that I'm not the one

who wants to waste valuable time telling this story,' Drake said.

'All right, all right, carry on,' said Mrs McMahon.

'The man laid the briefcase flat on my desk and opened it up. It was full of money. I'd estimate that there must have been in the region of one hundred thousand dollars in there. He said that the money was mine if I helped him in his quest,' Drake said.

'To find the Lazarus Key,' said Mrs McMahon.

'Yes, how did you know?'

'Because it'd be a pretty pointless story if he was looking for something else, wouldn't it?'

Drake coughed to cover up his embarrassment. 'Quite so.'

He drew something on a piece of paper and held it up for them to see. His back was to the door so that it was impossible for Colm to make out what it was.

'This is the Key,' Drake said, pointing to the picture he'd drawn. 'I had come across it before, although it was only mentioned briefly in text books. It was thought to be more of a myth or legend than a true relic. Something like UFOs or the Loch Ness monster. An interesting story, but unlikely to be true.

'There were rumours that there were three Keys originally,' Drake continued.

'What's that got to do with us?' Mrs McMahon asked.

'He's getting to that, Mom,' said Marie.

'Don't call me Mom. Your daughter may be American, but you're Irish. Call me Ma or Mammy.'

'Sorry, Ma.'

'Can we focus, please?' Drake said. 'Time is passing quickly and he will find us. The man has many resources at his disposal.'

'Go on, so.'

'The Key is mentioned in some historical texts along with its supposed powers.'

His voice was almost a whisper now and Colm had to strain to hear what he was saying.

'Naturally, as a man of logic and reason, I didn't believe in these so-called supernatural powers, but my research and the events of the last few days have made me change my mind. What I have uncovered has me worried. And this is vitally important. If you know how to use it, then whoever has the Key will not die. Ever. It is an evil thing. When your body fails you and you die as people normally do at the end of their lives, you will come back again. You will not be human, not as we know it, but you will live. Something in the Key – magic, something we do not understand – draws life from those around you. Hugh DeLancey-O'Brien, the last known holder of the Key, never died.'

'Of course he did. They buried him, didn't they?'

'You know the stories. When he died the maid took the Key in her hand. She died the following morning. All the life in her transferred into the Key and when it was buried with DeLancey-O'Brien he drew her life's power back into him. He rose again. He is not dead, he is not living, he is something in between.'

'So if I hold the Key in my hand ...'

'Then the creature that was once Hugh DeLancey-O'Brien will come and take it from you. But it isn't only the Key that he seeks, it is your life. The life that is held in the Key. It will sustain him and you will die.'

'The lesson then is not to hold the Key, isn't it?' said Mrs McMahon.

'Well, yes. Anyway, back to my visitor at the university. I couldn't understand why the man was so anxious to lay his hands upon it. Certainly it would be of some value to a museum or a collector of relics, but nothing in the region of the amount of money he was offering me to track it down. He told me he had been after it for many years, but no one had been able to find it for him. He said I was his last hope. I accepted his offer. I was intrigued and it was far too much money to turn down. I spent the night researching the Key and uncovered some interesting points about it, but nothing concrete. Then I got lucky. At least at the time

I thought it was luck. I showed my evening's work to Marie. She recognised the Key for what it was immediately. She had heard stories about DeLancey-O'Brien and a secret society when growing up. And in her youth she had read *The Book of Dread*, the account of a poor unfortunate who had searched for the Key.

'I now realised how dangerous the Key was and I regretted accepting the man's offer, but even then I didn't realise what a black valley it would lead me to. The man himself knew something of the Key – that it had been in the possession of a secret society in Boston some time in the 1800s. They were a powerful sect, but no one knew how they maintained that power. A more evil bunch of villains never existed. Their leader lived for an exceptionally long time, longer than anyone had any right to live and he held the city in his iron grip.

'That is until the Key was stolen by someone as treacherous as them. Someone who joined the gang and under cover of night robbed the Key. They believed he was an Englishman and for decades afterwards they sent members of the society to England scouring the country for the traitor who had taken their precious relic. They never found that man.'

'Because he was here,' said Lauryn. 'It was Hugh DeLancey-O'Brien.'

'He stole it. The blackguard,' Mrs McMahon said. 'He was the type all right. There were plenty of stories about him. Even when I was growing up. And he died a long time before I was born.'

'Except he didn't die,' said Drake.

·◆·

The Brute stirred as if waking from a marathon sleeping session. He yawned and stretched his arms. He had stopped sweating. In fact, he was feeling a lot better than he had in hours. The sickness had passed. He still felt weak and he didn't feel up to standing yet. For some reason he thought of Colm. Where was his cousin? He half-remembered him leaving the room and saying he'd be back in a minute. And had he tried to lift him on to the bed? He wasn't sure if they were memories or dreams. Maybe he'd just lie here for a few more minutes even though some part of his brain, something deep down, was telling him to get up and go downstairs. Nah, he'd lie here. He didn't like being told what to do, even when it was his own mind doing the telling.

·◆·

Despite the situation he was in, Colm began to feel giddy. He almost had to stop himself from laughing. What was wrong with him? He wasn't enjoying this situation so why did he suddenly feel so good? He felt better than he had in ages. Weird.

'DeLancey-O'Brien made one mistake though. He didn't know how the Key worked. Not properly. That was his downfall. If he had understood it he would still be here today, living in this house. There were plenty who knew how to use it though. Over the years there have been rumours about the Key. Scrawled passages in ancient scripts. As far as we can tell there were originally three Keys. One was buried with Attila the Hun. Another was lost with Rasputin.'

Mrs McMahon looked at him blankly.

'He was a monk in Russia who had many enemies, but no matter how often they thought they had killed him he came back to life. He finally died beneath a frozen river. The theme of the river and ice is mentioned throughout all the accounts of the Lazarus Key. As far as I am aware it is only this that can destroy it.'

'So we have to find the Key and freeze the horrible yoke,' Mrs McMahon said.

'In a manner of speaking.'

'Well why couldn't you just say that in the first place instead of blathering on for hours about Rasputin and all sorts of nonsense. How do we get rid of it?'

Drake opened the freezer and took out a silver metal box no more than six inches square.

'We put it in this ice box and then we bury it deep beneath a river bed.'

'And that will stop the Key from working?'

'I hope so.'

'What do you mean you hope so? Will it or won't it?' asked Mrs McMahon angrily.

'I don't know. Until a week ago this Lazarus Key was just a fable to me. I thought it existed but, as I said, I didn't believe in its magical powers. I haven't slept since Marie told me about it. I've spent all my time researching and travelling until I knew everything about it. DeLancey-O'Brien may not have known how to use it properly, but I can guarantee you this man does. And I suspect he won't be using it for the good of the world. It's something that needs to be destroyed and we're the ones who are going to have to do it.'

'What about the creature? What if he comes after whichever of us has it? That means we're dead, doesn't it?'

Drake nodded. 'I'll take responsibility. I'll take the Key and hold onto it. If I don't destroy it in time and the creature comes after me, then one of you must try to finish the job.'

'You can't do that, Peter. You can't take that chance,' Marie cried.

'Rather him than one of you two,' said Mrs McMahon.

'Ma, leave him alone,' Marie said. She sounded stressed. 'Peter's only trying to help us.'

'Help us? He's the one who got us into this mess in the first place. The lanky streak of ditchwater.'

'It's not his fault,' Marie said. 'It was just a case of really bad luck.'

'Bad luck that you went to work for him. Bad luck that when you realised you were in terrible danger you came here. And just plain bad thinking that you brought poor Lauryn with you and put her right bang wallop in the middle of trouble. She's only a young girl,' Mrs McMahon said angrily.

'It's OK. I can handle myself. Good ole US of A toughness,' Lauryn said.

'Oh, shut your cakehole, Lauryn,' Mrs McMahon said. Her face softened. 'Sorry.'

'Forget it, Gran. We're all a bit worked up,' Lauryn said.

'Why didn't you just tell the man that you couldn't find it?' Mrs McMahon asked. 'Wouldn't that have been the sensible thing?'

'That's what we did. But then we got the feeling we were being watched. No matter what we did. No matter where we went,' Marie said.

'The man had people following us. He knew we were on to something. I don't know how he knew it, but he did,' Drake said.

'He knew it cos he's a genius and he's one of the most wanted men in America,' said Lauryn.

'Lauryn. Ssssh,' Marie said.

'Well, he is,' said Lauryn.

'We don't know that for sure. We think the man works for The Ghost. It's the nickname for one of the FBI's most wanted criminals. They don't have a real name for him. Nobody knows who he is.'

'It's serious then,' said Mrs McMahon.

'We pretended to go to work one morning, but we'd already decided. We snuck out the back door and met Lauryn ...'

'At Pizza Hut. I ditched school,' she said proudly.

'... and flew straight here. We thought that if the hotel was closed for a couple of days we might be able to search for the Key without anyone noticing. Our plan was to destroy it so that this evil man wouldn't ever get his hands on it. I hid out in a bed and breakfast and Marie persuaded you to go away on a trip.'

'I knew it wasn't rats. You closed the hotel for ye're own sake. There's never been a rat here in all my years,' Mrs McMahon shouted, almost joyfully.

'That doesn't matter right now.'

'It matters to me,' she huffed.

'You came back early and let the guests in before we had the chance to find it. We tried to protect them because we know the man will find us. Our only hope is that we get to the Key before he does. If he's that dangerous already I can only imagine what damage he's going to do if he gets the Key. And remember, he'll know how to use it properly,' Drake said.

Colm had to stop himself from crying out. So they weren't kidnapping him. They were hiding his family so this horrible man wouldn't find them.

Mrs McMahon looked at her daughter. 'I think I know where it is,' she said.

'Ma?'

'When I was a girl I got lost in the woods once. I came across an auld, I don't know what you'd call it, trapdoor. I heard my name being called out. As if it was from under the ground. I wanted to open the door and climb in there. I wanted to do it more than anything, but before I could, my father found me. He gave me a right leathering and told me never to go into that part of the woods again. He said bad things were in there and it was no place for a young girl.'

Drake picked up the piece of paper. 'Is this what you saw?'

Mrs McMahon grabbed the paper, crumpled it up and flung it towards the door.

'I told you already I never saw the blasted thing. I just said I know where it might be.'

The paper rolled across the floor and came to a stop when it bounced gently against the door. Colm checked that no one was looking, then grabbed the balled-up piece of paper. He opened it as quietly as he could and saw what Drake had drawn. The Lazarus Key. Only the name was misleading. It wasn't a key at all.

It was a diamond. With a skull inside. And it was in Colm's pocket.

Colm would have gulped except his body wouldn't allow it. He was still too happy. And now he knew why. Because like The Brute, like the man who had written *The Book of Dread*, he held the Key. And when you held the Key you were happy for a while. And then the sickness came. And then the creature came.

There was only one thing for it. He was going to have to see if Drake's plan to destroy the Key worked. But before he could do anything he saw Drake was looking in his direction.

'How long have you been there?' he asked coldly.

'Not that long,' Colm said. 'Listen, I have to tell you something ...'

He got to his feet. Now he could see that Drake wasn't addressing him. He was looking past him, to the man who stood behind him.

'I think he was talking to me,' said the rat-faced little man.

Fifteen

'Get out of my kitchen. In fact, get out of my hotel right now or I'll call the Gardaí,' said Mrs McMahon.

The rat-faced man just smiled, revealing pointed little teeth that reminded Colm of fangs.

'Don't you smirk at me,' said Mrs McMahon bravely.

She grabbed the saucepan from the kitchen floor and ran towards him waving it above her head.

'Take one more step and you, your family and everyone you've ever cared about will pay for it,' he said.

Mrs McMahon stopped in her tracks.

The man didn't have a gun or a knife. He didn't appear to have a weapon of any sort, but there was something in the cold, calm way he spoke that made Mrs McMahon realise he was telling the truth. He could hurt them all and he would if she didn't do what he was telling her. She hadn't been scared in years. She had no time for fear. But she was afraid now. All at once she understood why Drake and her daughter were so terrified of this man.

'How did you find us?' Drake demanded.

'You don't get to ask any questions, Mr Drake,' said the man.

'Don't hurt us,' Marie said.

'You don't get to tell me what to do either,' he said.

Colm smiled. He couldn't help himself. He knew that the situation was a grave one. He knew that the creature would soon be coming for him and that his one chance of destroying the Lazarus Key had disappeared since this strange, dangerous man had turned up, but he was still grinning like an eejit.

'Mrs McMahon, isn't it?' said the rat-faced man.

Mrs McMahon nodded.

'I believe you said you might know the location of the object I'm looking for. Is that correct?'

She nodded again.

'Then you're going to come with me,' he said.

'You can't take her out into the woods at this time of night. She's old. She won't be able to make it,' Lauryn cried.

The man looked at her, his eyes like slits. 'Are you telling me what to do?' he asked.

'No, sir,' said Marie, putting a protective arm around her daughter. 'She doesn't understand the situation.'

'I do understand it,' said Lauryn, shrugging her off. 'And I'm not letting you take my grandmother out there.'

The little man didn't say a word. He walked, almost silently, across the kitchen until he was standing in front of Drake and Marie. The professor's lower lip quivered.

'I-I-I,' he began.

He didn't get to finish.

The rat-faced man's arms moved in a blur of speed. Too fast for Colm to understand what he'd done, but half a second after he did whatever he did, Drake and Marie lay in a crumpled heap on the floor.

'What have you done?' Lauryn roared. She rushed to her mother's side.

'They're not dead,' said the man wiping the back of his hand on his jacket.

'Will she be all right?' Lauryn asked with a tremble in her voice.

'I don't know,' he replied. 'If she's not, then it's your fault.'

Lauryn was on the verge of tears.

'Mrs McMahon, we'll need a flashlight for our journey into the woods. Get one.'

She disappeared into a utility room and returned with a torch.

'I'm taking her with me now. I'll be back when we find the Lazarus Key,' the man said.

'And what happens then?' Colm asked.

'Why would I tell you?' he said. He almost smiled again, but changed his mind halfway through. 'Mrs McMahon. Lead the way.'

'I'll be fine, Lauryn. You look after your mother. Don't worry about me,' she said with a wink as she left the kitchen, the rat-faced man by her side.

There was silence for a few minutes after they left. Colm and Lauryn were in too much of a daze to speak.

He wondered what to do. He had the Key in his pocket. If he gave it to the rat-faced man he might just let them go. Or he might not. Wouldn't the creature come and get the man instead of him? The one person who could answer that question was lying unconscious on the floor.

And if he did hand over the Key then what powers would he be giving to the man? If the stories Drake told were true, then the consequences could be terrible. He could just try to destroy the Key in the metal contraption that Drake had taken from the freezer, but then what would the man do if he didn't get the Key? And there was the other problem. What would happen to him if he kept the Key in his pocket? The creature would come for him. No matter what way he looked at it things were bad.

He was shaken from his mood by the sound of sobbing. Lauryn was cradling her mother in her arms.

'She'll be OK,' Colm said even though he wasn't sure she would be. He just wanted to sound reassuring.

Marie gasped and inhaled a lungful of air.

'Mom,' Lauryn said, brushing a lock of hair from her mother's forehead.

'I'll be OK,' Marie said feebly. She didn't look OK. 'Is your Gran ...'

'She's fine,' Lauryn lied. 'She's just gone to ring the doctor for you.'

Marie smiled and closed her eyes.

'I'm going after him,' Lauryn whispered.

'No, you're not,' Colm said. 'I am.'

·◆·

The argument didn't last for long. No matter what he said he couldn't persuade Lauryn to stay. She's more stubborn than her grandmother, he thought.

'Are you sure you won't stay here with your mother?' he asked one last time.

Lauryn had placed a rolled-up towel beneath her mother's head. Marie's breathing was regular now and she looked like she was just sleeping. Drake was still out cold.

'My mom will be fine, but I'm not going to let my gran walk through the woods with that creep,' she said.

Colm knew he'd have to let her come with him. Time

spent arguing was wasted time.

'Where are my parents?' he asked.

'They're in the cellar,' Lauryn said. 'Do you want me to release them?'

He did, but he knew it wouldn't be a good idea. It would take ages to explain everything to them and even if they believed him they weren't going to let him go out into the night after a half-mad criminal and a … whatever the creature was.

'No, it's fine,' he finally replied.

'I'm sorry about locking them up,' she said. 'I …'

'I know. You just wanted to protect us. It would have been easier though if you'd just kicked us out of the hotel when we first arrived.'

'I tried to scare you off.'

'Yeah, I got that,' Colm said. 'Can you bring that metal thing that Mr Drake brought? And is there another torch as well?'

'Torch?'

'Flashlight,' Colm said, remembering that Americans had a different word for it. Lauryn kissed her mother on the forehead then grabbed a couple of torches from the utility room and stuffed them into a rucksack she'd found there.

'I think this belongs to Mr Jenkins,' she said. 'He'd go mad if he knew we had it.'

'Where is Mr Jenkins?'

'Locked up with your folks.'

Colm's dad wouldn't be happy to be stuck with the man who he thought had ripped him off. Of course being locked in a cellar wasn't going to put him in a good mood either.

Lauryn picked up the ice box. 'It's freezing,' she said as she stuffed it into the rucksack. 'Do you have a plan?'

'Of course I do,' he lied. 'OK, let's go.'

Lauryn said goodbye. Her mother didn't answer. She looked worried for a moment, then she seemed to put it to the back of her mind. Her face became a stern mask of resolve.

·◆·

They reached the front door of the hotel.

'They have at least a ten minute head start. How are we going to find them?' Lauryn asked.

'I don't suppose you know where they were going,' he said.

'No,' she replied.

Colm sighed. Were they defeated before they even started?

'I know,' The Brute shouted from the top of the stairs.

Sixteen

Carrying the Key was taking its toll on Colm. He felt dizzy from time to time and it was difficult to shake it off. He tried to concentrate, but it wasn't easy. He didn't feel right.

The Brute, on the other hand, was in good spirits. He almost had a spring in his step. Whether this was because he was feeling better or because he was finally getting his walk in the woods with Lauryn, Colm wasn't sure. All he knew was that it bugged him.

They'd been walking for twenty minutes and he wasn't convinced his cousin knew where he was going. He'd take a left and then suddenly turn back and go in the opposite direction. Then he'd turn back again saying that he was right the first time. He sensed that Lauryn was just as fed up as he was because she kept sighing and tutting, but she hadn't said anything. Not yet anyway.

The forest was dark and cold, and mist swirled about their knees. Colm felt like he was in a horror film. Some of the moonlight filtered down through the trees but they still needed the torches. Every so often the beams from the flashlights would land on a pair of black eyes and Colm's heart would leap into his mouth, but it always turned out to be a fox or a badger and it was just as spooked as he was.

They walked in silence, partly because there wasn't much to be said, but mainly because they were listening out for any sound of Rat Face and Mrs McMahon. Rat Face and Mrs McMahon. Sounds like a bad television series, Colm thought.

'Here,' The Brute whispered.

They stopped.

'Shine the torch over here. To my left,' he said.

He meant his right.

Twin beams alighted on a nest of broken brambles.

'I think this is where I first went wrong,' he said as quietly as possible. 'I broke down these thorns.'

'How far from here is the place?' Colm asked.

Lauryn slapped her hand against her forehead.

'What is it?' The Brute asked.

'I'm so dumb,' she said.

'No, you're not. Don't ever say that,' said The Brute before he'd stopped to think what he was actually saying.

'What? No, it's not a confidence thing. Just something I should have thought of earlier. How did you know where we were supposed to go?'

'I heard a noise outside and when I looked down from the hotel window I saw your grandmother and this weird little man going into the woods,' he said.

'But how did you know where they were going?' she asked.

'I just assumed they were looking for the chamber. The place where I was earlier.'

His face dropped. As if he'd blocked out his memory of his trip to the woods and now, in one horrible moment, he'd suddenly remembered everything.

'W-w-why are we going there?' he stammered. 'That place is awful. There's … we can't go there.'

'You were in there,' Lauryn gasped. 'So you saw the Key, didn't you? A diamond …'

'… with a skull inside,' The Brute said finishing her sentence. 'I think I'm going to puke.'

He didn't get sick, but he didn't look great either. It reminded Colm of a phrase his mother used. What was it? Oh yeah, she'd seen healthier corpses. Now why did he have to think of the word corpse at a time like this.

'Did you touch the Key?' Lauryn asked. Her voice was anxious.

'Yes,' he said.

'He took it,' Colm said.

'He what?'

'It wasn't my fault. I didn't mean to. I just … I felt … I had to take it. I don't know why. I just had to,' The Brute said.

'Where is it?' Lauryn asked.

'I have it,' Colm said.

'You what?'

'I said, I have it,' he repeated.

'I heard you the first time. I just couldn't believe my ears. Give it to me. Now.'

'What are you going to do with it?'

'I'm going to destroy it,' Lauryn said.

'Destroy it? Why? What is it?' The Brute asked.

'I'll explain later, Brute,' Colm said.

'Brute? There's no need to call me names.'

Colm felt like laughing. And crying. But he hadn't the energy for either. The sickness was consuming him and he hardly had the strength to keep going. He just wanted all this to be over and for things to go back to normal. Normal and boring. That seemed like the nicest thing in the world right now.

He reached into his pocket and took out the Lazarus Key. Lauryn grabbed it from him.

'Why didn't you tell us that you had it earlier?' she asked, annoyed.

'Because I didn't know what it was then. Not until Drake explained it in the kitchen. If you'd just told me what was going on instead of kidnapping us ...'

'Who was kidnapped?' The Brute asked.

'Not now, Brute,' Lauryn said in a fierce whisper.

'Everyone's at it,' he said huffily.

'If you destroy it then that man might go mad. You don't know what he'll do to your grandmother,' Colm said.

'He's not going to do anything to her. I won't let him,' Lauryn snapped, even though she didn't have a clue as to how she was going to stop him. 'We'll destroy it first, then I'm going to go after him.'

'Are you sure?'

'No. But we have to do it anyway,' she said coldly. 'Get the box out of the rucksack.'

She removed the rucksack from her shoulder and dropped it on the ground. Colm took out the ice box and carefully placed it in front of him. He unhooked the clasp. It opened with a hiss and a blast of cold air hit his face. It felt refreshing and for a moment his head felt clear again.

Lauryn paused for a second. 'Wish me luck,' she said.

'Good luck,' The Brute said grumpily.

She placed the Lazarus Key in the box and Colm closed

it quickly. Even the sight of the Key disturbed him, but it felt good not to have to carry it anymore.

'What do we do now?' The Brute asked.

'We wait,' Lauryn said.

·◆·

The creature stirred from the tomb that had been its home for almost one hundred and fifty years. Its skin was deathly white and waxy and clung to its skull as if had been painted on. A few thin strands of white hair were scraped across its head. An eye patch covered what had once been its eye; the other, blood red, protruded from its socket. Its mouth was as black as a Hallowe'en night. Its aged and torn robes clung to its skeletal frame with a rotten aroma of must and decay. Its feet, withered like dead leaves, scraped along the forest floor.

It made a hissing sound that might once have been laughter. It could almost smell the flesh. The life it would take tonight would be young and it would make it grow strong.

The creature that was once Hugh DeLancey-O'Brien stretched out a hand, more skeleton than flesh, and screamed in delight. It would not be long now.

·◆·

'How long has it been?' Lauryn asked.

Colm shone the torch on his watch. 'Ten minutes. How long did Mr Drake say it should take?'

'Only a minute,' Lauryn said. 'I think. But I thought the longer we left it in there the better the chance of it working.'

Three pairs of eyes stared at the box.

'Should we open it now?' The Brute asked.

'Guess so. You want to do the honours, Colm?'

Colm opened the box. Steam rose from it and mixed with the fog. It took a few moments to clear. They leaned in to get a better look. To their dismay the Lazarus Key was still there. Intact. Gleaming in the moonlight.

'Maybe it doesn't destroy it in the way we think it should,' Colm said.

'What do you mean?'

'I don't know. It mightn't disintegrate or anything, but its power could be gone.'

Lauryn was cheered by the thought.

'Yeah,' she said. 'You could be right. It's probably useless now.'

'Didn't Mr Drake say something about burying it beneath a riverbed? Maybe that's what we have to do?' Colm said.

'I agree,' said The Brute even though he didn't know what he was agreeing to.

'You're wrong,' said the rat-faced little man. 'Ice and rivers don't do anything to the Key. Mr Drake was mistaken in that. Although I would like to thank you for finding it for me.'

• ◆ •

'How did you talk me into this?' Cedric asked.

The car whizzed around the bend so fast that it crossed the white line and sped along the wrong side of the road. Luckily there was nothing coming.

'I know you, Ced,' Kate said. 'Deep down you're a good man. Really deep down. Deep as the Grand Canyon deep. Way down to the centre of the earth deep. Not on the surface. Deeper than …'

'I get it,' Cedric said through gritted teeth. 'By the way, you're wrong. I just want you to know that. If I was on my own I wouldn't be driving back to the hotel. I'm only doing this for you.'

'Ah, that's so sweet,' Kate said with a smile.

'Shut up.'

'You shut up.'

'So, what does your horoscope say about our chances?' he asked.

Kate picked up the tabloid newspaper from the floor and pretended to read.

'Taurus. Here we are. Today will bring an unexpected visitor that will shake you from your dull routine. Embrace the change,' she said.

'I was wondering more about whether we'll live or die,' he said.

'Chances of death – ninety per cent.'

'Excellent,' he said sarcastically.

·◆·

Once Lauryn had finished swearing there was a moment of quiet. A strange moment in which everything was still and peaceful. Everyone knew it wouldn't last.

Colm wondered how the rat-faced man had managed to sneak up on them like that. That's twice he's done it, he thought. A mute ninja would have made more noise than him.

'Is my grandmother OK?' Lauryn asked.

'She's alive. Or dead. I don't remember which,' said the man.

Lauryn would have attacked him if The Brute hadn't held her back. He had only ever seen the man from the bedroom window, but now that he was close to him he realised he was dangerous. He'd been in enough fights to recognise an opponent you didn't mess with.

'You win,' said Colm to the man. Despite his tiredness there was a twinkle in his eye. He took the Lazarus Key from the box and held it out in front of him. 'Take it.'

'I'm going to,' said the rat-faced man. 'But not yet.'

'What do you mean?' Colm asked.

'There's some hungry creatures in this forest. And it's feeding time,' he replied.

'I think he means the creature from the trapdoor,' said The Brute.

Yeah, I got that, thought Colm.

'I could just throw it away,' he said.

'You could,' said the rat-faced little man, 'but you won't. First of all, I won't let you. And secondly, it won't do you any good. Your energy and life have already transferred into the Key. They'll stay there until the creature comes and takes it or until the Key is destroyed. But that's not going to happen tonight. Not unless you're carrying a vial of hydrochloric acid with you.'

Hydrochloric Acid. Why was that familiar, Colm wondered?

The man cackled, then his face became serious again. 'You're going to hold it tight in your chubby fist until I tell you otherwise. You look like the sort of child who cares for his family and you know that if you don't do as I say, then there will be repercussions for them.'

He licked his lips and Colm almost gagged. He believed what the man had said. He was trapped and he knew it. He was going to have to do as he was told.

'What about you? What do you care about?' Lauryn cried.

The man didn't answer. He held a finger up to his lips.

'Ah,' he said. 'We have a visitor.'

·◆·

The creature smelled them. Four. Three young. One that held the Key. It moved slowly, its robes dragging through the mud. Its sense of anticipation was growing. The youth it would steal tonight would replenish it. It knew it. It could escape that wretched chamber, its home, its prison, forever.

It could hardly remember what it was like to be human. To drink cool, clear water. To eat fresh food. To feel the sun on its skin. It had been in darkness for what seemed like eternity and it longed for the light. It had been years since it had had a chance to escape. Decades since the last person had wandered by its lair. Then it had called out, but the person hadn't responded. Too strong perhaps. It needed someone foolish. With a mind it could manipulate. And then this evening the boy had come. The one with the confused mind. Those were the easiest ones. The ones that had no true sense of self. Only minutes now. It felt a hunger where its stomach used to be before it had dried up.

Soon it would be free and Hugh DeLanccy O'Brien would live again.

·◆·

Cedric slammed on the brakes and sent gravel flying. It pinged against the windows of the Red House Hotel. He got out of the car and ran to the front door, Kate just behind him. The door was open. Funny that, Cedric thought. Although he knew it wasn't funny. In fact, it sent a chill right through him. There was only one explanation. The rat-faced man was already here. He knew he wasn't that far away when he rang him, but he never thought he'd be here so quickly.

'Stay near me, Kate,' he said. He wished he had a gun. In America all the private detectives had guns. Well, they did in the movies anyway.

'Maybe we should split up. I'll take upstairs and you ...'

'I said to stick with me. I'm not letting you out of my sight. Not if he's around here,' Cedric said.

Kate felt her heart warm. He was a good man after all. She was right.

'Have you got a plan?' she asked.

'There's only one plan that makes any sense and that's to run away. Right now,' he replied.

'But we're not going to do that, are we?'

'No,' he said gloomily.

'Ced ...'

'Sssh. Do you hear that?'

'Yes. It sounds like someone crying. This way.'

They ran through the restaurant and into the kitchen.

Marie was sitting on the floor. She looked groggy. She held a glass of water up to Drake's lips, but he wasn't drinking. He was still out cold.

'Well, he's got his man. We may as well go,' Cedric said.

Marie looked up when she heard his voice.

'Who are you?' she asked. A single tear ran down her cheek.

'Us? We're nobody. Just looking for a room for the night, but you're obviously busy, so we'll be on our way,' he replied.

'Shut up, Cedric,' Kate said. 'Is everything all right?'

'Does it look like everything's all right?' Marie asked.

Kate had to admit that it didn't. It looked far from OK.

'The children,' Marie said. 'I think they're gone into the woods after him. Please help us. He has to be stopped.'

Cedric Murphy didn't need to ask who had to be stopped. He already knew.

·◆·

Colm heard the rustle of the leaves. The creature was getting closer. It got colder all of a sudden. It might have been the lateness of the hour or just a coincidence, but he didn't think so.

'Keep your eyes peeled children. You're about to see something amazing,' smirked the rat-faced little man.

The Key felt warmer in Colm's hand. It was almost burning now as he grew weaker by the second. His breath came in ragged bursts. Maybe Lauryn was right after all, he thought. If you touch *The Book of Dread* you don't survive to see another day. Why wasn't The Brute doing something, he wondered. He was a man of action. At least that's what he'd always told Colm. He looked over at his cousin, whose face couldn't hide what he was feeling. He was petrified. Lauryn wasn't any better. Her hands trembled. Her face was ghostly pale in the beam of the flashlight.

'Hey. Kids. Are you in there somewhere?'

A man's voice. Off to the right. Colm hadn't the strength to respond.

But The Brute and Lauryn had.

'Over here.'

'Help. Please help.'

'If either of you speak another word then I will end this right now,' said the rat-faced little man quietly.

They shut up immediately.

·◆·

'Where did the voices come from?' Cedric asked.

'Just over there,' Kate replied.

'If we just ... euurrggh.'

'Ced. Are you OK? Speak to me.'

'I'm fine. I just stepped into something slimy and … ah, man, my shoes are ruined. And some of it's on my pants leg. This is my best suit,' he said forlornly.

'Ced. Focus.'

'Right. This way.'

He ran as fast as he could, but it was difficult to run through a forest at night with only a torch to guide the way. And Cedric was quite useless when it came to any form of exercise. Mainly because the last time he'd had a proper workout was in a PE class in primary school over thirty years previously.

'I think I see something,' Kate said.

·•◆•·

The creature couldn't see it, but it knew it was near. It could taste it. Only minutes separated it from a new life. The world would be different now. But it would adapt. It didn't matter what century it was. Humans never changed. Victory always came to the strong and the intelligent. Never the weak. Never the stupid. And it was going to be strong again. As strong as when it too had been human. People feared it. He could sense it. But they had feared it then too. When it had owned the house and land and everything around. It was coming home. Soon now.

·•◆•·

'What is it?' Lauryn screamed.

She grabbed The Brute by the arm. A few hours ago this would have made him the happiest teenager in the country, but now he didn't even notice. He didn't answer. He just stood, staring at the creature that slowly crossed the clearing.

Colm could barely keep his eyes open, but they were open just enough to see the miserable, foul thing that was coming for him.

·◆·

'Quickly, Kate,' Cedric said when he heard Lauryn's scream.

'I can't,' Kate said, gasping in great lungfuls of air. 'You go on, Ced. Help them. I'll catch up with you.'

Even though Cedric wasn't speedy, he was faster than Kate. He burst through the briers, the thorns ripping at his clothes. This time he didn't give his suit a second thought. He had to help the children. The light from his torch bounced around picking out parts of trees and the ground until it landed on a shape. Someone lying on the ground. He bent down. She was breathing. An old woman. It was Mrs McMahon.

·◆·

'Stop screaming,' commanded the rat-faced little man, but

for the first time in a long time one of his commands was ignored.

Lauryn couldn't stop. She had heard about the creature, but seeing it was far worse than she imagined it ever could be. It made her recoil in horror. In panic.

'Get it away from me,' she shouted. She shut her eyes. She couldn't bear to look at it.

But she didn't have to worry. It wasn't going towards her. Colm was its prey.

The creature stretched out a long miserable arm and hissed one word.

'Miiiiiinnnnne.'

It chilled Colm to the bone. He had to get away from it. But he couldn't get up. His mind willed him to but his body refused to obey its instructions. The creature that was once Hugh DeLancey-O'Brien shuffled towards him. It was less than ten yards away.

The rat-faced little man smiled. Then the smile changed to a frown, as The Brute roared and, with his head down, charged like a bull at the creature. He was right on course. Full speed ahead.

He missed.

He didn't know how. The creature didn't even appear to move, yet somehow it had evaded him. He'd get it the second time. He wouldn't miss twice.

He wouldn't get the chance.

The rat-faced little man grasped The Brute's neck between his thumb and forefinger and The Brute slumped to the ground.

'Lauryn,' Colm said.

She didn't hear him. She was too busy screaming.

He took a deep breath and felt the pain in his chest.

'Lauryn,' he shouted.

This time she heard him. She stopped in mid-scream, her face a mask of confusion and terror.

'Run,' he whispered.

She snapped out of it. Just like that. The old Lauryn was back.

The creature was five yards away.

'No. I won't run. I'm not leaving you.'

'Very admirable,' said the little man, with a mocking laugh.

Time seemed to stand still. Colm's mind raced. There had to be something he was missing. What was it? The Key. No. Holding the Key. Whoever held the Key. And something else. Something he'd read. In *The Book of Dread*. The creature hated light. That was it.

He lifted the torch. His hand shook, but he managed to focus and shone it at the thing that was moving towards him. It hissed. It didn't like the light. But it didn't stop it. It shuffled closer and closer. Colm willed the sun to rise above the trees and kill the creature, but dawn was still twenty minutes away.

He couldn't go out like this. Just sitting there doing nothing. Think, Colm, think, he said to himself. There had to be something. Some clue. Something he'd heard. Something he'd read.

The rat-faced little man sat down beside Colm.

'Not long to go now,' he said.

He was so close to Colm that their shoulders were touching. Well, at least if the creature gets me then he'll get this man as well, Colm thought.

'He won't touch me,' the man said, as if reading Colm's mind. 'The problem with Mr DeLancey-O'Brien over there,' he nodded in the creature's direction, 'is that when he stole the Key in Boston he didn't know how to use its power. I do. The knowledge was passed down by the Sign of Lazarus from generation to generation. We knew one day that the Key would return to us. I will rid the world of this vile creature. Unfortunately for you, you will have to lose your life in the process.'

The rat-faced little man had never spoken that much in his entire life. He rubbed the tattoo on the inner part of his arm. The diamond with the skull inside. The symbol of the Lazarus Key. The symbol his father, grandfather and beyond had tattooed on their arms, all hoping one day to be the one who would return the Key to what they regarded as its rightful home. And now the moment was here.

Colm tried to clear his mind of worry and fear. It didn't work. But from somewhere, the idea popped into his head. Just like that. And he knew at once what he had to do. It was so simple. It was also difficult. He was only going to get one chance. If he failed then it was all over. And even if he succeeded he didn't know if it would work.

He needed Lauryn. She was clever, wasn't she? He was about to find out.

The rat-faced little man watched with glee as the creature loomed over Colm. He'd waited almost forty years for this moment. Ever since the day his father had shown him the tattoo of the skull and the diamond on his arm. He'd told him the story of the gang in Boston that every generation of his family had belonged to and how that Englishman – although he now knew he was Irish – had stolen their most powerful possession. The one that made them rulers. The thing that made them great. He had vowed then and there, even though he was only nine years old, that he would recover the Lazarus Key and that one day he would use it and that he would be as powerful as his ancestors had been. And now that moment had come.

'Lauryn. The library. Do what you did in the library,' Colm said, his voice barely above a whisper.

The rat-faced man had let his guard slip for the first time in years. He'd been too wrapped up in his thoughts. That wasn't like him. Had the boy said something? It didn't matter. What could he do now?

Colm didn't know if that was enough for her. He hoped so. He couldn't waste any more energy. He needed to save what little he had.

'I told you not to speak,' said the man.

The creature leaned over Colm as if it was going to envelop him in its robes. Colm felt its icy touch and his blood ran cold. His eyelids fluttered. There wasn't long left now.

The rat-faced man spotted something out of the corner of his eye. A movement. It was the girl.

Lauryn dived through the air. Straight for him.

The man didn't even try to stand up. He just swatted her away as if she was a fly that was buzzing around his head. Lauryn landed face down in the mud.

The rat-faced little man threw back his head and laughed. Long and loud.

With his last drop of strength Colm swung his arm around and slapped the man right in the mouth.

'What do ...' the man began. There was something in his mouth. What had the boy done?

Lauryn was on her feet in a flash. She knew what Colm had done.

She jumped onto the rat-faced man's back and clamped her hand tightly around his mouth. The man was stunned. Nobody had ever fought back. Ever. He'd show her why.

He threw himself backwards and slammed her into the ground. She cried out in pain, but clung on to him. There was no way she was letting go.

The object rattled around in the man's mouth. He couldn't spit it out. He tried to sit up, but Lauryn dragged him back down. The force sent the object flying to the back of his throat and it lodged there. The man coughed and spluttered. He was choking. His eyes began to water, but he didn't panic. He never panicked. He did the only thing he could think of – he swallowed the object.

He could breathe again. He shrugged Lauryn off. That was better.

'I warned you,' he said. He balled his hand up into a fist. He was going to have to teach that child a lesson. No, it didn't matter now. He could do that in a minute. The creature had the boy. He had to watch this first.

But then the thing that was once Hugh DeLancey-O'Brien released its grip on Colm and turned around. It looked straight into the face of the rat-faced man. The man frowned. A puzzled look on his face.

'What are you doing? The boy has the Key, not me, you idiot.'

'No, I don't,' Colm whispered.

'But.' Slowly it dawned on the man. The stupid child had thrown the Key into his mouth. And he'd swallowed it.

His eyes bulged and the tiniest wisps of smoke escaped from the gaps between his teeth.

'The only thing that can destroy the Key ...' Colm began.

There was no need for him to finish. The man knew what he was talking about. He was smart like that.

Question: What type of acid is the main acid in your stomach?

Dad: Hydrochloric Acid.

The creature reached out for him.

'Uh-oh,' said the rat-faced man. He wanted to run, but the Key was drawn to the creature and he couldn't move. Not a muscle.

Colm and Lauryn shut their eyes as the creature wrapped its wretched frame around the man. It had to have the Key. No matter what.

The rat-faced little man's screams rang throughout the woods.

'Don't look at him,' Colm called out.

'Not a chance,' Lauryn replied.

The screams seemed to last for an eternity, but eventually

there was silence and when they finally opened their eyes the creature was gone. The rat-faced man lay on the ground. He looked as if he'd aged forty years in the last minute. He was still breathing, but he didn't move.

'Is he ...' Lauryn began.

'No, he's still alive,' Colm said.

The first rays of sunlight broke through the trees.

'We did it,' Lauryn shouted in delight. Then she saw Colm's face. 'Didn't we?'

'The creature is still out there.'

'But it doesn't have the Key.'

·◆·

The creature knew what had happened. It was defeated. But not permanently. The man it had taken wasn't young and it was only able to get partial replenishment as it could not grasp the Key in its hand, but it had enough power to return to its chamber. There it would lie and wait. The Key it had stolen was gone forever, but there were two more out there somewhere in the world. It was certain of it. And somehow the Key would find its way to its chamber. All the creature had to do was wait.

·◆·

Colm tried to get to his feet, but he stumbled and fell back onto the mud. He was too weak. The swing had taken the very last bit of his energy.

'We have to stop the creature getting back to its ... lair,' he said.

'Where is it?' Lauryn asked.

'I don't know,' he said. 'He does.'

He pointed towards The Brute.

Lauryn leaned over Colm's cousin and slapped him on the face. He groaned.

'Hey, what's your name. Brute. Wake up. We need your help,' she said.

'Whazzat?'

He shook his head groggily.

'He's out of it,' Lauryn said. 'What are we going to do?'

•◆•

The creature was almost back at its chamber. The sun was growing stronger and although the trees offered it some protection it needed to get back underground. It could see the door now. It was close.

Lauryn's voice echoed through the woods. 'Is anyone there? Stop the creature. If anyone can hear me – stop it now.'

Foolish child, the creature thought. It couldn't be stopped.

'Is this a fancy dress party? Because if it isn't then you're making a horrible fashion statement,' Cedric Murphy said, stepping out from behind a tree.

The creature hesitated. Who was this fat thing blocking its path?

Cedric shoved the trapdoor shut with his mud-covered Italian loafer. It closed with a loud bang. The creature glided towards him. It was weak now. The patches of sun were drawing away the strength it had taken from the rat-faced man. It reached out and grasped Cedric by the shoulder.

He felt an icy chill run through him. His lips turned blue and his teeth began to chatter. All the strength in his legs went and he collapsed right on top of the trapdoor as the sun's rays filtered through the trees and on to his prone body. Even though he was too unconscious to realise it, Cedric had taken away the creature's last hope of survival. His immense weight was too much for it to move and it could not get back into its chamber.

·◆·

The creature screamed in rage. Smoke curled up from its robes. It was dying. All those years underground. All that waiting. It made no difference now. Its time was at an end. And as the sun's rays pierced its body the creature that was once Hugh DeLancey-O'Brien saw the morning light for the first time in over one hundred and fifty years.

Its dried-up old body began to wither in the light and by the time Cedric Murphy woke up several minutes later there was no trace of it to be found.

•◆•

Colm was feeling better. He knew he was on the mend because he was starving. He'd have given anything to have a double cheeseburger, chips and curried beans even though it was only half-past five in the morning.

He felt even better when Lauryn returned with Cedric Murphy. They'd checked the underground chamber and found it was empty. Lauryn had said it was a cold and horrible place and she never wanted to see it again as long as she lived.

Cedric had introduced himself and Kate as Bill and Jill, two tourists who just happened to pass by at the right moment, and having made sure everyone was all right they quickly said their goodbyes. It was only after they left that Colm wondered why they had turned up at the hotel in the middle of the night. Still, that wasn't something for him to worry about now. He'd been through enough already and his brain hurt. A lot.

There had been an awkward moment while he had waited for Lauryn to return. The Brute, who was more or less back to his old self, had checked that Colm was OK. They'd both stood there, unsure of what to say, even though after all they'd been through in the previous twelve hours Colm thought that it should have been easy for them to talk to each other.

Finally, he'd broken the silence.

'Thanks for, you know, trying to stop the thing, the, ahm, creature, from attacking me,' he'd said.

'No problem,' The Brute had replied. He hadn't looked at Colm. He must have found his trainers very interesting because he'd kept staring at them.

Silence.

'That creature. Sort of a mad thing, wasn't it? Like something from a movie,' The Brute had said.

'Yeah. Mad all right.'

'Yeah.'

They were both glad when Lauryn appeared.

Seventeen

Colm was both delighted and terrified when his parents were finally released from the cellar. Delighted because they were safe and sound and no matter how much they bugged him – and they bugged him a lot – they were his parents and he loved them. Usually he loved them because, well, he had to, but not now. He was actually pleased to see them.

The terrified part wasn't going to be any trouble until later on when he'd receive the lecture of all lectures, no doubt to be followed by the punishment of all punishments. At least he wouldn't have to tell them about the creature. It'd be enough for them to think that some dangerous criminal had been on the loose and that he'd been caught up in the middle of it all, but if he told them about a … he wasn't sure what to call it … some sort of zombie … well, whatever it was, they'd either punish him more severely for making it up or if they believed the story they'd have to be hospitalised for shock. Either way, it wouldn't be good.

His mother grabbed him in a bear hug and smothered him with kisses. He could see Lauryn smirking in the corner. But then he looked again. She wasn't smirking, she was smiling. And to his great delight, The Brute got the same treatment. He didn't seem to mind too much. He supposed that after all they'd been through a few kisses weren't going to be that much of an embarrassment.

His father ruffled his hair and gave him a friendly thump on the shoulder. It hurt.

There was lot of talk after that. Too much of it. All he wanted to do was have a nice meal and a long sleep, but there was questions followed by questions and just when he thought they'd run out there were a few more.

His parents took a lot of convincing that Mr Drake wasn't a kidnapper and that he was only trying to protect them, but once Mrs McMahon was given the all clear by the doctor she managed to persuade them. She wasn't too happy when his father peppered the conversation with the words 'sue you for everything you've got', but from the glint in his father's eye Colm knew he wasn't serious.

Mr Drake would have to spend the night in hospital, but the doctor said that this was just a precaution and that he expected him to make a full recovery. After that, the paramedics carried the rat-faced man to an ambulance. The driver had asked if anyone knew him. He'd presumed that the man must have been somebody's grandfather as he looked as if he was over eighty years old. When the Gardaí had turned up Marie told them that the man was on the FBI's Most Wanted list. They seemed very interested in that, although they were going to have some difficulty in identifying him.

They wanted to take statements from Colm and The Brute, but Mrs McMahon told them that the boys had been locked up in a separate room and hadn't seen anything. The sergeant seemed suspicious, but since the man they were after was already under arrest, he let it go.

A couple of hours later all the commotion had died down and Mrs McMahon brought them into the restaurant and insisted that they all have a cup of tea and a full Irish breakfast served by Mr Jenkins.

The Brute said he wasn't hungry, but as soon as he smelled the sausages cooking in the kitchen he realised he was ravenous and he ate everything that was put in front of him. There wasn't much conversation at the breakfast table. Everyone was too tired and had spent long enough talking already. Colm was glad of the silence.

Eventually they finished up and Mr Jenkins brought their bags to the car.

'He'd better not be expecting a tip,' Colm's father said.

'Everything's on the house,' Mrs McMahon said.

'I should think so too,' Colm's mother replied. She didn't seem quite as taken with the Red House Hotel as she had been on first viewing.

Before they got into the car Lauryn came over to say her goodbyes.

'Sorry for the mess guys,' she said.

'No problem,' said The Brute shyly.

'Sorry about making you dive at the man like that,' Colm said.

Lauryn smiled. There were still some traces of dirt on her face from where she'd landed in the mud. 'That's cool. You knew he'd get the better of me, didn't you?'

'Yeah. Sorry.'

'I'd have done the same in your position.'

'Is it gone do you think? The Key?' Colm asked.

'I talked to Peter, Mr Drake, before the ambulance took him away. He can't believe that he didn't realise the acid would destroy it. He said he'd misread the notes. The Key wasn't a real diamond. It was made out of some special material. The acid would have dissolved it in seconds,' Lauryn replied. 'I still can't believe you thought of it.'

'Just luck,' Colm said. 'What's going to happen here now?'

'I guess the hotel's not going to be re-opening for a while. I don't think anyone will want to stay here once word gets round about a dangerous gangster turning up in the middle of the night,' Lauryn said.

'Would have been better if it was just rats here, not rat-faced men,' said The Brute.

Lauryn laughed and he turned bright red. 'Good one. My gran is still in a bit of shock. She knew all the stories about the Key, but she never believed they were real. She does now. Kind of a weird night, huh?'

'The weirdest,' Colm said, but right now it didn't seem strange at all. He knew that was just because of the tiredness. Once he'd had a couple of good night's sleep he'd probably freak out about it. He smiled to himself.

She shook his hand. 'Thanks for everything, kid.'

'Lauryn?'

'Yeah?'

'Please don't call me kid,' he said.

'Thanks for everything, Colm.'

'You're welcome,' he replied.

'Wow, you sure are polite. Even after all we've been through.'

She turned to The Brute. He wouldn't look her in the eye.

'See ya, tough guy,' she said.

'See ya,' he mumbled.

She winked at Colm then leaned forward and kissed The Brute on the cheek. Instant glow. Two hundred degrees of heat.

'I-I-I ...'

'Bye,' she said and ran back into the hotel.

'Well, that was ...' Colm began, but The Brute interrupted him.

'If you make a smart remark I'll hit you so hard ...'

'No. You won't. You won't hit me.'

The Brute looked at him. There was something different about his cousin. Something he almost ... Oh no. He didn't like him, did he? That'd be awful.

They got into the car and his father drove off at somewhere between five and seven miles an hour. Slowly, very, very slowly, the Red House Hotel began to fade into the distance.

'Now, Michael,' Colm's mother said.

'Huh,' grunted The Brute.

'What are we going to tell your mother? Because we can't tell her the truth. She'd have my guts for garters,' she said.

The Brute pricked up his ears. Here was a chance.

'I don't know, Auntie Mary. I'd hate to lie to my mother. Unless we could come to some sort of arrangement of course.'

Colm relaxed into the seat and closed his eyes. Yep, in less than an hour The Brute would be out of his life and things would be back to normal. Just him, his mam and his dad again. Within a minute he was snoring and even his cousin didn't dare wake him up.

Epilogue

The car journey back to Dublin was long and boring and quiet. Just the way Kate wanted it to be. She was exhausted and didn't mind the fact that Cedric hadn't said a single word for over an hour. He hadn't even complained when she'd smoked the last of her cigars and the acrid smoke had filled the small car. When he did speak it wasn't what she had expected to hear.

'I'm going on a diet,' he said.

'A diet? Why?'

'Why do you think?' Cedric replied, patting his ample belly.

'You're fine the way you are.'

Cedric lapsed into silence.

'What are you thinking, Ced?'

'Lots of things,' he said, too tired to make a sarcastic

remark. 'The Lazarus Key was real. I hadn't even considered that it might have been real. I should have. A good detective has an open mind, always expects the unexpected. What happened tonight ...'

'Nobody could have guessed what was going to happen,' Kate said.

'The Key brought that creature back to life. You didn't see it, Kate. It was a horrible, wretched, pitiful thing. I'd prefer to be dead than to live a half-life like that.'

'What do you think it was? A zombie?'

'I don't know what you'd call it. Giving it a name doesn't change anything. I put those children in danger.'

'You helped them when it counted,' Kate said.

Cedric grunted.

'Listen, Ced. You did the right thing in the end and it's all over now, isn't it?'

'Yes, it's over,' he smiled. They'd got out of there before the Gardaí had arrived. Nobody knew who they were and he was certain none of the adults or children were going to say anything.

'What about the rat-faced man? Is he going to recover?' she asked.

'Nope. He's a goner. The Ghost is no more.'

'The Ghost? He was The Ghost?'

'Yeah. Had to be. He had the time and money to come

over here to search for the Key. He was powerful too, I could tell that when I met him. He was the most terrifying individual I've ever come across. Yep, he was The Ghost all right. He had all he needed, except for one important thing. Like everyone else he was going to grow old and die.'

Kate got it. 'But he thought that if he got the Lazarus Key he could live forever.'

'He was wrong.'

'Wow, you're a brilliant detective.'

'I am,' Cedric agreed, already putting his mistakes behind him.

'If he was The Ghost, then that means we're safe, doesn't it? I mean The Ghost was a secretive man. He'd never tell anyone his plans, so nobody knew he was over here. There's nobody who's going to come looking for him. We're in the clear.'

Cedric thought about it. She was right. They were in the clear. He could put all this behind him and start afresh. And this time he wasn't going to make any mistakes. He was going to be the best detective he could be.

•◆•

12 Hours Later

In a cabin in the foothills of the Blue Ridge mountains, deep in the heart of America, a man sat on an old wooden chair, calmly waiting for the telephone to ring. He glanced at his watch just at the moment the phone chirped into life. Right on time. He smiled a thin-lipped smile. No one ever kept him waiting. He answered the call.

'Speak,' he commanded.

The person on the other end of the line sounded nervous, jittery. 'It's bad news, I'm afraid.'

The man felt the familiar rage bubbling just beneath the surface. He had a vicious temper, but had long since learned to control it. All it took was self-discipline and the man was the most disciplined of them all.

'Should I go on?' asked the voice on the phone.

'Yes.'

'Mr Smith is dead.'

There wasn't even a flicker of emotion on the man's face. Nothing to show that this news bothered him. So that was it – his brother was dead. The idiot. He was always too eager to put himself in the way of danger, the man thought. His brother was a stupid man – a stupid, little rat-faced man.

They didn't look like brothers. The man in the cabin was tall and had delicate, almost pretty, features. In spite of this people didn't like him. Something about his eyes. Something that hinted at the cruelty that lay just beneath the surface. His eyes were colder than a shark's.

'Are you still there?' the voice on the phone asked.

'Yes.'

'I have some details. He passed away at the Red House Hotel, a small hotel in Ireland. His last known contact was a detective in Dublin. Cedric Murphy. And there were some guests and staff in the hotel. Six adults and three children. I have their names here. Will I read them out?'

'No, put the names and details in an envelope and leave them in the usual pick-up spot. I'll have them collected.'

'Sorry for your loss.'

The man hung up without replying. His brother was dead. What did that make him feel? Nothing. He didn't love his brother. He didn't even like him. But family was family. His death would be avenged. He wouldn't allow the one who had caused it to get away with it. That wouldn't be right.

He rolled up his shirt sleeve and looked at the tattoo on the inside of his arm. The Lazarus Key. His brother had always wanted to find the Key.

The man who was The Ghost stood up and stretched his arms. So, he was going to Ireland. All other business could be put on hold for now. He had a lot of work to do and it was only just beginning. First he would find the man called Cedric Murphy, then he would track down everyone who was involved in his brother's demise and he would make them pay. He would make them all pay.